ALMOST
FAMOUS WOMEN

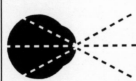

This Large Print Book carries the
Seal of Approval of N.A.V.H.

ALMOST FAMOUS WOMEN

STORIES

MEGAN MAYHEW BERGMAN

THORNDIKE PRESS
A part of Gale, Cengage Learning

GALE
CENGAGE Learning·

Farmington Hills, Mich • San Francisco • New York • Waterville, Maine
Meriden, Conn • Mason, Ohio • Chicago

GALE
CENGAGE Learning·

LIBRARY OF CONGRESS CATALOGING-IN-PUBLICATION DATA

Bergman, Megan Mayhew.
  [Short stories. Selections]
  Almost famous women : stories / Megan Mayhew Bergman. — Large print
edition.
    pages cm. — (Thorndike Press large print peer picks)
  ISBN 978-1-4104-7957-0 (hardback) — ISBN 1-4104-7957-9 (hardcover)
  1. Large type books. I. Bergman, Megan Mayhew. Pretty, grown-together
children. II. Title.
PS3602.E7556A6 2015
813'.6—dc23   2015010806

Published in 2015 by arrangement with Scribner, a division of Simon &
Schuster, Inc.

Printed in Mexico
1 2 3 4 5 6 7 19 18 17 16 15

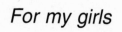

For my girls

'Tis the white stag, Fame,
we're a-hunting,
bid the world's hounds come to horn!

— EZRA POUND

You can fill up your life with ideas and still
go home lonely.

— JANIS JOPLIN

CONTENTS

9

New York denies Violet Hilton, pictured with Daisy, a marriage license, on the grounds that it would be illegal to issue the license to two persons (1934). **Associated Press photo, July 5, 1934. Reprinted with permission.**

The Pretty,
Grown-Together Children

Let me tell it, I said.

No, you're a liar and a drunk, she said. Or I said.

Our voices could be like one. I could feel hers in my bones, especially when she sang — a strong quicksilver soprano. We were attached at the hips and shared blood, but no vital organs. Four arms, four legs — enough to make a man give a second look.

One of us has to tell it, I said, and it's going to be me.

An agent had come to see us. Or that's what he claimed to be. A talent scout. I couldn't remember his name. He wore a blue sports coat with heavy gold buttons, jeans, loafers. His hair shone with tonic, and he knew how to shake hands. My bones ached from his grip.

Look, I said to Violet. I'm a better storyteller than you. You sing, I tell stories.

Violet didn't answer. She'd vanished, the

13

way the great Harry Houdini had taught us to do in the RKO Studios cafeteria. When you're tired of each other, he'd said, imagine retreating into an imaginary shell. A giant conch. Harry was short and bowlegged. His curly hair splayed across his forehead into a heart shape. Separate *mentally,* he'd said.

What about when Daisy is indiscreet? With men? Violet had asked. What do I do then?

Same thing you've done in the past, I'd said. Look away.

Violet was like that. Made her voice rise when she wanted to play innocent. She pretended to be shy. But I could feel her blood get warm when she spoke to men she admired. I could feel her pulse quicken.

Back in the RKO cafeteria days, we had floor-length raccoon coats, matching luggage, tortoiseshell combs, and high-end lipstick. We had money in the bank. We took taxis. We traveled, kissed famous men. We'd been on film. The thirties, forties, even the fifties. Those had been our decades. We had thrived.

In the RKO days, people thought our body was the work of God.

But now we were two old showgirls bagging groceries at the Sack and Save in Aberdeen. There were no more husbands, no boyfriends. Just fat women and their dirty-nosed children pointing fingers in the grocery line.

Can y'all help us get these bags out to the car, they'd ask.

I never met so many mean-hearted women in my life. Violet and I were still able-bodied, but we were old. Our knuckles hurt from loading bags. Our knees swelled from all the standing. But we'd do it to keep our boss happy, hauling paper bags to station wagons in the parking lot.

I jes' want to see it walk, the kids would whisper.

We lived behind the grocer's house in a single-wide trailer with a double bed and a hot plate. Mice ran through the walls, ate holes in our cereal boxes.

Look, the agent said. I'm going to come back tomorrow and we're going to talk about some projects I have in mind.

Come after supper, I said.

Houdini had told us: never appear eager to be famous.

The agent came closer. His cologne was fresh. He made Violet nervous, but not me. He reached for each of our hands and kissed our knuckles.

Until then, he said, and disappeared through the screen door. The distinctive sound of the summer night rushed inside. Cicadas, dry leaves rattling in the woods, a single car on the dirt road.

Some nights Violet and I sat on the cinder-block steps outside, rubbing our bare toes in the cool dirt, painting our nails. Like most twins, we didn't have to talk. We were somewhere between singular and plural.

After the agent left, Violet and I sat on an old velour couch, turning slightly away from each other as our bodies mandated. I forgot how long we'd been sitting there. There were framed pictures of people we didn't know on the walls. The kitchen table had three legs. One had been chewed and hovered over the linoleum like a bum foot. The curtains smelled like tobacco. The radio was tuned to a stock car race.

Rex White takes second consecutive pole.

Violet was still, hands on her knees. She was probably thinking about an old boyfriend she had once. Ed. Violet had really loved Ed. He was a boxer with a mangled face and strange ears that I didn't care for. He wasn't fit for a star, I told her. When she went into her shell I figured that's who she went there with.

I was hot and dizzy. Our trailer had no air-conditioning.

Postmenopausal, I figured. I needed water.

16

I stood up.

Violet came out of her imaginary shell.

We have to get some money, she said, as we moved toward the sink. We have to get out of here. I have paper cuts from the grocery bags. My ankles are swollen. How come you never want to sit down?

I'm working on it, I said. Besides, we're professionals. We've got something left to offer the world.

I let the faucet sputter until the water ran clear.

One of us could die, I said. And they'd have to cut the other loose.

So that's what it takes, Violet said and disappeared into herself again.

I was told our mother was disgusted when she tried to breastfeed us.

Just a limp tangle of arms and legs. Too many heads to keep happy, Miss Hadley said. Lips everywhere. Strange cries.

Miss Hadley was our guardian. We lived with her in a ramshackle house that was part yellow, part white — an eyesore on the nice side of town. The magnolia trees were overgrown and scratched the windows. The screened-in porch was packed with magazines, rusted bikes, broken lamps, boxes of old clothes and library books.

Weren't for me you'd be dead, Miss Hadley said. I *saved* you.

Like stacks of coupons and magazines — we were one of the things Miss Hadley collected, lined her nest with.

Once, when you was toddlers, you got out the door nekkid and upset the neighborhood, she said. She liked to remind us, or maybe herself, of her generosity. Her ability to *tolerate.*

Carolina-born, Miss Hadley looked like she was a hundred years old. Her cheeks sank downward. She had a fleshy chin and a mouthful of bad teeth.

Daisy, she'd say, I'm fixin to get after you.

And she would. She once threw a raw potato at my forehead when she found me rummaging in the pantry after dinner. Miss Hadley slapped my knees and arms with the flyswatter when I talked back. Sometimes she'd get Violet by accident.

She ain't do nothing to you, I'd say. Leave her be.

Don't sass me, she'd say. You've got the awfulest mouth for a girl your age.

When we were young, Violet and I had the thickest bangs you'd ever seen, enormous bows in our hair. There were velvet ribbons around our waists, custom lace

18

dresses, music lessons. We were almost pretty.

We learned how to smile graciously, how to bask in the charity of the Christian women in the neighborhood. We learned to use the toilet at the same time. We helped each other with homework and chores.

Miss Hadley kept a dirty house, scummy dishes in the sink. There was hair on the floor, toilets that didn't work, litters of rescued dogs that commanded the couch. Her stained-glass windows were cracked. The front door was drafty. Entire rooms were filled with newspapers. Her husband was dead (if she'd ever really had one) and she had no children except for us. Looking back, we weren't her children at all. We were a business venture.

We fired the shotgun at Beaufort's Terrapin Races, presented first place ribbons at hog and collard festivals. We tap-danced with Bob Hope. We crowned Wilson's tobacco queens, opened for the Bluegrass Boys at various music halls. We knew high-stepping cloggers, competitive eaters, the local strong men. We knew showmanship.

I remember my line from the Terrapin Races: *And now, ladies and gentlemen, the tortoise race.* Years later, when I woke up in the middle of the night in a hot flash, that line would come to me.

We didn't know to be unhappy. Violet and I — we didn't know we were getting robbed blind. We didn't know about all the money we'd made for Miss Hadley.

I don't charge you rent, she said at the dinner table. But I should charge for those hungry mouths.

We believed ourselves to be in her debt. We were *grateful,* even.

Miss Hadley's yard was overgrown with ivy, honeysuckle, and scuppernong vines. When we hated what she'd made for dinner — she was a terrible cook — we'd go out hunting scuppernongs, eat them fresh off the vine. I liked them best when they looked like small potatoes, soft, golden, and dusty. I had to tug Violet out the front door to eat them. If we came in smelling of fruit, Miss Hadley would come after us with the switches.

Ya'll been eating scuppanons again, she'd say, catching the backs of our legs. Scuppy-dines is for poor kids.

We lived in what had been the maid's room, behind the kitchen. We shared a double bed, slept back-to-back. There was a poster of President Hoover tacked to the wall. Violet papered our drawers with sheet music and hid licorice in her underwear.

Miss Hadley had lined the room in carpet samples. I kept a cracker tin full of movie stubs and magazines.

Violet and I lay in bed at night talking about the latest sheet music, or a boy who had come with his parents to see us play at the music hall. We talked about lace socks, traveling to Spain, how we'd one day hear ourselves on the radio, learn to dance beautifully with a partner on each side.

I want to waltz, Violet said.

I want a new dress first, I said. Or to sing "April in Paris" onstage.

Teaching you to walk was some ugly business, Miss Hadley often said. Dancing — I can only imagine. You girls need to work at sitting still, staying pretty. That's why you've learned to read music.

Violet and I — we had thick skin.

We slept with an army of rescued greyhounds, lithe and flea-bitten, in our bed at night. We fed them dinner rolls, put our fingers on their dull teeth, let them keep us warm.

There were no secrets. Imagine: you could say nothing, do nothing, eat nothing, touch nothing, love nothing without the other knowing.

Like King Tut's death mask, we were exhibited.

The calling card, as I remember it: "If we have interested you, kindly tell your friends to come visit us." *The Pretty, Grown-Together Children.*

There were boxes of these in Miss Hadley's basement, a few scattered across the kitchen table. Stacks in every grocery store and Laundromat in town.

Hear the twins sing "Dream a Little Dream of Me." Hear the twins recite Lord Byron's "Fare Thee Well."

Miss Hadley sat us on a piano bench or leather trunk to play our instruments. We crossed our legs at the ankles. She set out a blue glass vase, which she instructed visitors to deposit money into.

I took in these girls out of the goodness of my heart, she'd say, and I'd appreciate you donating from the goodness of yours so that they can continue their music lessons.

Bless your hearts, the ladies would say, coming up close to inspect us.

Children would ask: Does it hurt? Do you fight? You think about cutting that skin yourself?

It did not hurt to be joined — we knew no difference. As for fighting, yes, but we were masters of compromise: *I'll read books now if you'll go walking later. You pick the movie this week and I'll pick next. We can get in bed but I'm going to keep the lamp on so I can read. We can sleep in but you owe me a dollar.*

At night, our legs intertwined. This was not like touching someone else's leg. It wasn't like touching my own, either. It was comforting, warm. We were, despite our minds' best efforts, one body.

You kick, Violet told me. You dream violent dreams.

Your arms twitch, I said, though it wasn't true.

After Miss Hadley's death, when the movers began emptying her house, our flyers were used to protect the dishes. We were wadded up and stuffed into teacups. Our advertisements scattered across her dry yard. Scuppernongs lay bird-picked and smashed on the lawn. The greyhounds were leashed to the front porch. I could see the sun shining through the translucent skin on their heels. I remember thinking — what now?

When Miss Hadley got the fever we were

willed to her cousin Samson like a house. I'm afraid to tell you about the kind of man he was, how our skin got thicker. I'll tell you this. His house was dark, unpainted, and smelled of pipe smoke. Samson did not shower or shave. He didn't parade us in public or charge to hear us play music. In fact, the music lessons stopped. He kept us inside. He had other interests.

C'mere, sweetmeats, he used to say, patting his lap.

Ya'lls never been loved properly, he'd say.

There were months when we did not leave the house other than for school and church. It occurred to us to be depressed about our situation, scared. This was the first time we had been truly unhappy.

We were sixteen. One night we packed a bag of our best clothes, her saxophone, my violin. We waited until Samson was good and drunk, then snuck out the back door and caught a bus to New York. We'd never moved so fast together, never been so in sync.

The bag is heavy, Violet said. And my feet hurt in these pumps.

It's worth every blister, I said. Trust me.

Each step I thought of his breath. Each step I thought of his fingers. The pain went away.

We made it to the station, sweating in our high heels with turned ankles and empty stomachs.

Violet and I swore, in the backseat of that bus to New York, that we'd never mention Samson again. We'd pretend the things he'd done had never happened. The bruises on our thighs would heal and the patches of our hair would grow back. Until then we'd wear hats. We'd practice music on our own. We'd get back into the business.

When we couldn't pay the bus driver, he dropped us off at the police station. We were freezing. We'd never had a jacket made to fit us.

Put on your lipstick, I said to Violet.

I still like to think of that dime-store lipstick. It was soft and crimson and made me feel beautiful.

Excuse me, I said to a man smoking a cigarette on the cement steps.

He looked up at us in disbelief. He wore a three-piece suit and a tweed cap. His lips were full, and it hurt me to watch him sink his front teeth into his bottom lip.

I could see my breath in the air. The sound of New York was different than the sound of Miss Hadley's backyard. The street looked wet; there were bricks everywhere, lights lining the sidewalks. We were petri-

fied. I could feel Violet's blood pressure rising.

I never seen something so pretty and so
strange, he said.

And that's how we got hooked up with
Martin Lambert.

The agent will be back tomorrow, I said to
Violet.

I can't read this if you're going to keep
pacing, she said, trying to get through an
old copy of *Reader's Digest* while I bustled
about the bedroom.

Our bed in the grocer's trailer had one set
of threadbare sheets and a pale pink quilt. I
picked at the frayed edges when I couldn't
sleep.

Are you eating another cookie? I asked.

Old stock, Violet said, crumbs on her
mouth. Someone has to eat them. Grocer
was going to throw them out.

Our cupboard was filled with dented soup
cans and out-of-date beans. The grocer let
us take a bag of expired food home at the
end of each week.

I noticed the lines around Violet's eyes. I
guessed they were around mine too. Our
skin was getting thinner, our bones fragile.

Help me get this suitcase on the bed, I
said.

Violet used one hand to help.

Between us we had one brown leather suitcase full of custom clothes. There were dresses, bathing suits, pants, and night-gowns. Those we'd had for decades were moth-eaten and thin.

We've gotta mend these, I said. And not get fat.

No one's looking, she said, her mouth full of stale oatmeal cookie.

The agent is looking, I said.

This wasn't the first time Violet had tried to sabotage our success. Once, she'd dyed her hair blond. Then she tried to get fat. Every time I turned around in the forties she was eating red velvet cupcakes.

Your teeth are gonna go blood red from all that food coloring, I warned.

We had enough strikes against us in the looks department. One of Violet's eyes sloped downward, as if it might slide off her face. I hated that eye. I felt like we could have been more without it. Like Virginia Mayo or Eve Arden or someone with a good wardrobe and a contract or two.

Give me the cookies, I said. We can't show up naked. We can't show up in grocery aprons.

Violet held the cookie box in her right arm. I could let her have it, tackle her, or

27

run in a circle. I was too tired for the game. We'd played it enough as kids.

Fine, I said. Eat your damn cookies.

We each had talents. Violet could disappear inside her imaginary shell. I could go without food for days.

Martin Lambert had intended to take us to his sister's house that first night in New York.

I can't have you home with me, he said. We'll figure something out.

He flagged down a cab.

I can't feel my feet, Violet whispered.

I wasn't sure we'd ever been up so late before. The lights of the Brooklyn Bridge pooled in the East River. The people on the sidewalks wore beautiful jackets. Soldiers were home with girls on their arms, cigarettes on their lips. Restaurants kept serving past midnight.

I hoped Violet wouldn't tell him it was our first cab ride. The stale smell of tobacco oozed from the upholstery. Martin lit another cigarette and rubbed his palms on his pants. He kept looking at us out of the corner of his eye. Staring without staring. Disbelief. Curiosity.

I wanted to be close to him. I wanted to

smell his aftershave, touch the hair under his cap.

We sing, I said. We can swim and roller-skate, or play saxophone if you like.

Well I'll be, he said. Showbiz twins. Working gals.

Martin shook his head and chewed his lip. One thing I'd learned — people saw different things when they looked at us. Some saw freaks, some saw love. Some saw opportunity.

Violet was quiet.

We want to be in the movies, I said.

How old are you? he asked.

Eighteen, I lied.

I pulled the hem of my dress above my knees.

Violet jabbed me in the ribs.

Honest, I said.

Violet placed a hand over her mouth and giggled.

Cabbie, Martin said. Stop at McHale's. Looks like we're going to grab ourselves a few drinks.

Our hats were out of style and out of season, but we were used to standing out in a crowd.

Martin rushed over to a stocky man standing by the bar.

Ed, he said. I want you to meet Daisy and Violet.

Ed nodded but didn't speak. The two men turned to lean over their beers and talk quietly.

I felt a hundred eyes burning my back.

Look at the bodies, not the faces, I told myself.

Miss Hadley had said: Learn to love the attention. You don't have a choice.

There is no one in the world like you, I said to myself.

The spotlight is on, Violet said.

There is no one in the world like you.

We should find a hotel, Violet said. Then go back south tomorrow. If we leave early, we could get to Richmond. Even Atlanta. Somewhere *nice.*

With what money? I asked her.

One gin and tonic later I pulled Violet onto the stage. The band was warming up. We could be seen and gawked at, or we could be appreciated, marveled over. I knew which I preferred.

The first night Martin and I slept together, Violet said the Lord's Prayer eighteen times.

. . . hallowed be thy name. Thy kingdom come, thy will be done . . .

Violet!

30

On Earth as it is in Heaven.

Just keep going, I said.

Are you sure? Martin asked.

Violet had her hand over her eyes, a halfhearted attempt not to watch. She kept her clothes on, even her shoes.

Yes, I told him.

The room was dark but Martin kept his eyes closed. He never kissed me on my mouth. Not then, not ever.

During the day, Violet and I worked the industrial mixer at a bakery. We shaped baguettes in the afternoons. Nights, we sang at McHale's. I began drinking. Ed and Martin sipped scotch at a corner table, escorted us back to our efficiency in the thin morning light.

We primped for our performances like starlets. In the shower, we rotated in and out of the water. Lather, turn, rinse, repeat.

Let's go for a natural look tonight, Violet said, sitting down at the secondhand bureau we'd turned into our vanity table.

I was thinking Jezebel, I said. Red lipstick and eyes like Dietrich.

It looks better when we coordinate, Violet said.

I painted a thick, black line across my eyelid.

Let me do yours, I said, turning to her.

Some nights I felt like a woman — the warm stage lights on my face, the right kind of lipstick on, the sound of my voice filling the room, Violet singing harmony. Some nights I felt like two women. Some nights I felt like a two-headed monster. That's what some drunk had shouted as Violet and I took the stage. Ed had come out from behind his table swinging.

We were the kind of women that started fights. Not the kind of women that launched ships.

It took one year and a bottle of Johnnie Walker for Ed to confess his love to Violet.

Can you, um, read a newspaper or look away? he asked me.

I folded the newspaper to the crossword puzzle and chewed a pencil.

I been thinking, Ed said. You are a kind woman. A good woman.

Violet touched his cheek.

Does anyone know a four-letter word for Great Lake? I asked.

I watch you sing every night, and every night I decide that one day I'm going to kiss you, he said.

Violet cupped the back of his neck with her hands.

Erie, I said. The word is Erie.

An hour later and they had moved to the bed. I watched the clock on the wall, recited Byron in my head.

Ed cried afterward, laid his mangled face on Violet's chest.

I cried too.

When the agent comes, I said to Violet, let me do the talking.

We were taking a sponge bath in front of the kitchen sink, naked as blue jays. It was too hard getting in and out of a shower these days.

A cicada hummed somewhere in the windowsill.

Do you need more soap? Violet asked.

This is my plan to get us out of here, I said. We'll offer him the rights to our life story. We can get by on a few thousand.

I dipped my washcloth into the cool water and held it between my breasts.

Violet touched the skin between us.

We'll be okay, she said. I don't want you to worry.

Martin had never stayed the night. He had a wife. I wondered what she was like, what she'd think of the things we did.

Normal people don't do what you do in

bed, Violet said.

Since when are we normal? I asked.

You could keep your eyes closed, I said.

And my ears, Violet said, blushing.

Martin is a man's man, I told her. He knew what he wanted.

He was rough, sometimes clutching my neck or grabbing my hair. Afterward he'd talk about the movies we'd get into, how he'd be our agent.

The Philadelphia Story, he said, but instead of Hepburn, there's Daisy and Violet.

Then he'd wash his hands, rinse his mouth, wet his hair down, and leave.

One month my period was late.

Jesusfuckingchrist was all Martin would say.

In bed at night I asked myself what I would do with a baby. What Violet and I would do. I convinced myself we could handle it. We had many hands.

Ed slept over those days. I watched Violet stroke his hair, trace the shape of his strange ears with her fingertip. She slept soundly on his chest.

One night Martin dragged us to an empty apartment around the corner from Mc-Hale's.

Stay here, he said, backing out of the door.

A man came in — my body aches when I

34

think of it. He opened a bag of surgical instruments, spread a mat onto the floor.

Lie down, he said. Put your legs up like this.

I wanted to do right by Violet, keep Martin happy.

There was blood. Violet fainted. I no longer felt human. I felt as if I could climb out of my body.

We're done here, the man said. You shouldn't have this problem again.

We didn't leave our bed for weeks.

Martin disappeared.

He found the straight and narrow, Ed said. That operation of yours cost him two months' salary. He's somewhere in Cleveland now.

Ed brought us soup and old bread from the bakery while I recovered.

He continued to drink at the corner table nights when Violet and I sang. He was anxious, protective.

One night, after we'd performed "Tennessee Waltz," the bartender waved me over.

We've got leftover birthday cake, Daisygirl, he said, pouring me a gin and tonic.

I ate half a sheet cake between songs.

Daisy, Violet said. That's disgusting.

I pushed my empty glass forward for a refill.

The great Houdini told us to retreat to an imaginary shell when we got tired of each other, I said to the bartender, rolling my eyes at Violet.

We never met Houdini, Violet said.

Next thing I knew, Violet was wrestling my finger out of my mouth in the bathroom stall.

Stop it! she said.

You drink too much and you never eat, she said. What did you have yesterday? Half a peanut-butter sandwich? An apple?

We sank back against the wall of the bathroom stall. I still remember the pattern of the tile. Mint-colored rectangles with black squares. Ice cream, I thought. Tile like ice cream.

And the lying, Daisy, she said. The lying.

I watched ankles and shoes walk by the stall. Some women had beautiful ankles. Some women moved on two feet instead of four.

I still had icing on my fingers.

I need to stay here for a while, I said.

Violet held her hand underneath the stall door and asked a pair of ankles for a glass of water.

She had chutzpah when I least expected it.

Two weeks later, she surprised us all by dropping her panties into the church time capsule.

Did I ever tell you about our big break? I asked the agent.

I pulled out a stock photo Violet and I had autographed.

Violet and I might be broke and we might be strange but we were not ordinary.

Why do you have that old thing out? Violet asked. What are we — seven or eight?

She was eating saltines out of a dented tin box.

Can't whistle now, she said, smiling.

I pinched her bottom.

The agent is here, I whispered.

I'd once seen Violet cover my half of the photo with her hand to see what she looked like alone. We'd both wondered.

Here's how we ended up back in Carolina. I'd been in talks with a man who said he needed us for some public relations work.

It's like this, he had said. You show up at the theater and do an introduction for my movie.

We have to take the risk, I'd said to Violet.

But we don't, she'd said. We're old. We're retired.

We can't live on what we have, I'd said. Not for long, and I plan on living a long time.

We fronted him money for travel arrangements. He promised a hefty return. But what he did was leave us stranded at the bus station. We had no money, no car, only our suitcase.

I'm tired of trusting, Violet had said.

We'd cried that night, propped up against the brick station wall. A minister had taken us in, fed us hot dogs, said he knew of a local grocery that needed an extra pair of hands.

We have those, I said.

One night Violet shook me awake. Ed was in the bathroom with the door closed.

Get up, she said, switching on the bedside lamp. Get up.

Your eye, I said.

Violet had a red handprint across her face.

We stumbled to the dark kitchen.

He's drunk, she said.

Doesn't matter, I said.

I picked up the silver pot we used to boil noodles in one hand, grabbed a paring knife in the other.

Ed came into the kitchen crying.

Get out, I said.

I shielded Violet with my body, backed her up to the sink.

I flipped on the kitchen light. We all winced.

Leave, I said.

You're crazy, he said, sinking to his knees. Violet?

He'd said something else. What was it that he said?

I slung the silver pot into his crooked nose.

I can't picture what the agent looks like, I said to Violet.

Violet was reading the jokes in *Reader's Digest* and eating outdated yogurt.

There was the one in Texas, I said. And then the one in the city. The one with the Buick.

We're in Carolina now, she said. Why don't you rest?

When the agent comes back, we should do a number, I said.

There hasn't been an agent here, Violet said. You have a fever.

The one in the blue sports coat, I said. With gold buttons.

Do we have health insurance? she asked,

the cool back of her hand against my forehead.

When the agent comes back, I said, let's
do "April in Paris."

Let me get you a cool washcloth, she said,
lifting me gently from the couch.

Let the water run clear, I said. Tomorrow . . .

Trust God on this one, Violet said. Rest.

In our early days, people had trusted God's
intent. We were the way we were because
He made it so.

I remembered what Ed had said that night
I crushed his face. His mangled, fighter's
face.

You are not made in His image, he'd said.
You can't be.

*And now, ladies and gentlemen, the tortoise
race.*

My eyes watered. I felt as though I could
no longer stand.

I jes' want to see it walk.

I'm sorry, I said to Violet, before I pulled
her to the ground.

*If we have interested you, kindly tell your
friends to come visit us.*

There was something about the body, our
seam. Were we one or were we two?

I touched the skin between us.

One day soon, I said, you'll walk out of here alone.

Hush, Violet said. Hush.

Get a new dress, I said. Eat all the god-damn cookies you want.

M. B. "Joe" Carstairs, the fastest woman on water.
Photo reprinted with permission of The Mariners' Museum, Newport News, VA.

THE SIEGE AT WHALE CAY

Georgie woke up in bed alone. She slipped into a swimsuit and wandered out to a soft stretch of white sand Joe called Femme Beach. The Caribbean sky was cloudless, the air already hot. Georgie waded into the ocean and as soon as the clear water reached her knees she dove into a small wave with expert form.

She scanned the balcony of the pink stucco mansion for the familiar silhouette, the muscular woman in a monogrammed polo shirt chewing a cigar. Joe liked to drink her morning coffee and watch Georgie swim.

But not today.

Curious, Georgie toweled off, tossed a sundress over her suit, and walked the dirt path toward the general store, sand coating her ankles, shells crackling underneath her bare feet. A lush, leafy overhang covered the path, which stopped in front of a cinder-

45

block building with a thatched roof.

Georgie looked through the leaves at the sun overhead. She lost track of time on the island. Time didn't matter on Whale Cay. You did what Joe wanted to do, when Joe wanted to do it. That was all.

She heard laughter and found the villagers preparing a conch stew. They were dancing, drinking dark rum and home-brewed beer from chipped porcelain jugs and tin cans. Some turned to nod at her, stepping over skinny chickens and children to refill their cans. The women threw chopped onions, potatoes, and hunks of raw fish into the steaming cauldron, the inside of which was yellowed with spices. Joe's lead servant, Hannah, was frying johnnycakes on a pan over a fire, popping pigeon peas into her mouth. Everything smelled of fried fish, blistered peppers, and garlic.

"You're making a big show," Georgie said.

"We always make a big show when Marlene comes," Hannah said in her low, hoarse voice. Her white hair was wrapped. She spoke matter-of-factly, slapping the johnnycakes between the palms of her hands.

"Who's Marlene?" Georgie asked, leaning over to stick a finger in the stew. Hannah swatted her away and nodded toward a section of the island invisible through the dense brush, where a usually empty stone house covered in hot pink blossoms stood. Joe had never explained the house. Now Georgie knew why.

She felt an unmistakable pang of jealousy, cut short by the roar of Joe pulling up behind them on her motorcycle. As Joe worked the brakes, the bike fishtailed in the sand, and the women were enveloped in a cloud of white dust. Georgie turned to find Joe grinning, a cigar gripped between her teeth. She wore a salmon-pink short-sleeved silk blouse, and denim cutoffs. Her copper-colored hair was cropped short, her forearms covered in crude, indigo-colored tattoos. "When the fastest woman on water has a six-hundred-horsepower engine to test out, she does," she'd explained to Georgie. "And then she gets roaring drunk with her mechanic in Havana and comes home with stars and dragons on her arms."

"I've never had that kind of night," Georgie had said.

"You will," Joe had said, laughing. "I'm a terrible influence."

Joe planted her black-and-white saddle shoes firmly on the dirt path to steady herself as she cut the engine and dismounted.

"Didn't mean to get sand in your stew,"

Joe said, smiling at Hannah.

"Guess it's your stew anyway," Hannah said flatly.

Joe slung an arm around Georgie's shoulders and kissed her hard on the cheek. "Think they'll get too drunk?" she asked, nodding toward the islanders. "Is a fifty-five-gallon drum of wine too much?"

"You only make rules when you're bored," Georgie said, her lithe body becoming tense under Joe's arm. "Or trying to show off."

"Don't be smart, love," Joe said, popping her bathing suit strap. The elastic snapped across Georgie's shoulder.

"Hannah," Joe shouted, walking backward, tugging Georgie toward the bike with one hand. "Make some of those conch fritters too. And get the music going about four, or when you see the boat dock at the pier, okay? Like we talked about. Loud. Festive."

Georgie could smell butter burning in Hannah's pan. She wrapped her arms around Joe's waist and rested her chin on her shoulder, resigned. It was like this with Joe. Her authority on the island was absolute. She would always do what she wanted to do; that was the idea behind owning Whale Cay. You could go along for the ride or go home.

Hannah nodded at Joe, her wrinkled skin closing in around her eyes as she smiled what Georgie thought was a false smile. She waved them off with floured fingers.

"Four p.m.," Joe said, twisting the bike's throttle. "Don't forget."

At quarter to five, from the balcony of her suite, Joe and Georgie watched the *Mise-en-scène,* an eighty-eight-foot yacht with white paneling and wood siding, dock. Georgie felt a sense of dread as the boat glided to a stop against the wooden pier and lines were tossed to waiting villagers. The wind rustled the palms and the visitors on the boat deck clutched their hats with one hand and waved with the other.

Every few weeks there was another boat-load of beautiful, rich people, actresses and politicians, piling onto Joe's yacht in Fort Lauderdale, eager to escape wartime America for Whale Cay, and willing to cross a hundred and fifty miles of U-boat-infested waters to do it. "Eight hundred and fifty acres, the shape of a whale's tail," Joe had said as she brought Georgie to the island. "And it's all mine."

Georgie scanned the deck for Marlene and did not see her. She felt defensive and child-ish, but also starstruck. She'd seen at least ten of Marlene's movies, and had always liked the actress. She seemed gritty and in control. That was fine on-screen. But in person — who in their right mind wanted to compete with a movie star? Not Georgie. It wasn't that she wasn't competitive; she was. Back in Florida she'd swum against the boys in pools and open water. But a good competitor always knows when she's outmatched, and that's how Georgie felt, watching the beautiful people in their beautiful clothes squinting in the sun on-board the *Mise-en-scène.*

Joe stayed on the balcony, waving madly. Georgie flopped across the bed. Her tanned body was stark against the white sheets.

"Let's send a round of cocktails to the boat," Joe said, coming into the room, a large, tiled bedroom with enormous windows, a hand-carved king bed sheathed in a mosquito net. Long curtains made of bleached muslin framed the doors and windows, which were nearly always open, letting the hot air and lizards in.

"I'm going to shower first," Georgie said, annoyed by Joe's enthusiasm.

Joe ducked into the bathroom before heading down and Georgie could see her through the door, greasing up her arms and décolletage with baby oil.

"Preening?" she asked.

"Don't be jealous," Joe said, never taking her eyes off herself in the mirror. "It's a waste of time and you're above it."

Georgie rolled over onto her back and stretched her legs, pointing her painted toes to the ceiling. She could feel the slight sting of sunburn on her nose and shoulders.

"My advice," Joe called from the bathroom, "is to slip on a dress, grab a stiff drink, and slap a smile on that sour face of yours."

Georgie blew Joe a kiss and rolled over in bed. It wasn't clear to her if they were joking or serious, but Georgie knew it was one of those nights when Joe would be loud and boastful, hard on the servants. Maybe even hard on her.

The yacht's horn blew. Joe flew down the stairs, saddle shoes slapping the Spanish tile. Hannah must have given the signal to the village, Georgie thought, because the steel drums started, sounding like the plink plink of hard rain on a tin roof. It was hard to tell if it was a real party or not. Joe liked to control the atmosphere. She liked theatrics.

"Hot damn," she heard Joe call out as she jogged toward the boat. "You all look *beautiful.* Welcome to Whale Cay. Have a drink, already! Have two."

Georgie finally caught sight of Marlene, as Joe helped her onto the dock. She wore all white and a wide-brimmed straw hat. Even from yards away, she was breathtaking.

My family wouldn't believe this, Georgie thought, realizing that she could never share the details of this experience, that it was hers alone to process. Her God-fearing parents thought she was teaching swimming lessons on a private island. They didn't know she'd spent the last three months shacked up with a forty-year-old womanizing heiress who stalked around her own private island wearing a machete across her chest, chasing shrimp cocktails with magnums of champagne every night. A woman who entered into a sham marriage to secure her inheritance, annulling it shortly thereafter. A woman who raced expensive boats, who kept a cache of weapons and maps from the First World War in her own private museum, a cylindrical tower on the east side of the island.

"They'd disown me if they knew," Georgie told Joe when she first came to Whale Cay.

"My parents are dead and I didn't like them when they were alive," Joe said, shrugging. "Worrying about parents is a waste of time. It's your life. Let's have a martini."

As she listened to the sounds of guests downstairs fawning over the mansion, Georgie had trouble choosing a dress. Joe had ordered two custom dresses and a tailored suit for her when she realized Georgie's duffel bag was full of bathing suits. Georgie chose the light blue tea-length dress that Joe said would complement her eyes; the silk crepe felt crisp against her skin. She pulled her hair up using two tortoiseshell combs she'd found in the closet and ran bright Tangee lipstick across her mouth, all leftovers from other girlfriends, whose pictures were pinned to a corkboard in Joe's closet. Georgie stared at them sometimes, glossy black-and-white photographs of beautiful women. Horsewomen straddling Thoroughbreds, actresses in leopard-print scarves and fur coats, writers hunched artfully over typewriters, maybe daughters of rich men who did nothing at all. She couldn't help but compare herself to them, and always felt as if she came up short.

"What I like about you," Joe had told her on their first date, over lobster, "is that you're just so *American.* You're cherry pie and lemonade. You're a ticker tape parade."

Georgie loved the way Joe's lavish attention made her feel — exceptional. And she'd pretty much felt that way until Marlene put one well-heeled foot onto the island.

Georgie wandered into Joe's closet and looked at the pictures of Joe's old girlfriends, their perfect teeth and coiffed hair, looping inky signatures. *For Darling Joe, Love Forever.* How did they do their hair? How big did they smile?

And did it matter? Life with Joe never lasts, she thought, scanning the corkboard. The realization filled her with both sadness and relief.

On the way downstairs to meet Marlene, Georgie realized the lipstick was a mistake. Too much. She wiped it off with the back of her hand as she descended the stairs, then bolted past Joe and into the kitchen, squeezing in among the servants to wash it off. Everyone was sweating, yelling. The scent of cut onions made Georgie's eyes well up. Outside the door she could hear Joe and Marlene talking.

"Another one of your girls, darling? Where's she from? What does she do?"

"I plucked her from a mermaid tank in Sarasota."

"That's too much."

"She's a helluva swimmer," Joe said. "And does catalog work."

54

"Catalog work, you say? Isn't that dear."

Georgie pressed her hands to the kitchen door, waiting for the blush to drain from her face before walking out. She took her seat next to Joe, who clapped her heartily on the back.

The dining room was simply but elegantly furnished — whitewashed walls and heavy Indonesian teak furniture. The lighting was low, and the flicker of tea lights and large votives caught on the well-shined silver. The air smelled of freshly baked rolls and warm butter. Nothing, Georgie knew, was ever an accident at Joe's dinner table — not the color of the wine, the temperature of the meat, and certainly not the seating arrangement.

She'd been placed on Joe's right at the center of the table. Marlene, dressed in white slacks and a blue linen shirt unbuttoned low enough to catch attention, was across from Joe. Marlene slid a candle aside.

"I want to see your face, darling," she said, settling her eyes on Joe's. Georgie thought of the ways she'd heard Marlene's eyes described in magazines: *Dreamy. Smoldering. Bedroom eyes.*

Joe snorted, but Georgie knew she liked the attention. Joe was incredibly vain; though she didn't wear makeup, she spent time carefully crafting her appearance. She liked anything that made her look tough: bowie knives, tattoos, a necklace made of shark's teeth.

"This is Marlene," Joe said, introducing Georgie.

"Pleased to make your acquaintance," Georgie said softly, nodding her head.

"I'm sure," Marlene purred. "I just love the way she talks," she said to Joe, laughing as if Georgie wasn't at the table. "I learned to talk like that once, for a movie."

Georgie silently fumed. But what good was starting a scene? If I'm patient, she thought, I'll have Joe to myself in a matter of days.

"I'm sure Joe mentioned this," Marlene said, leaning forward, "but I ask for no photographs or reports to the press."

"She has to keep a little mystery," Joe explained, turning to Georgie.

"Is that what you call it?" Marlene asked, exhaling. "I might say sanity."

"I respect your privacy," Georgie said, annoyed at the reverence she could hear in her own voice.

"To reinvention," Joe said, tilting her glass toward Marlene.

"It's exhausting," Marlene said, finishing her glass.

Aside from Marlene, there were eight other guests at dinner — including Phillip, the priest Joe kept on the island, a Yale-educated drunk, the only other white full-time inhabitant of the island. There were also the others from the boat: Clark, a flamboyant director and friend of Marlene's; two financiers and their well-dressed wives, who spoke only to each other; Richard, a married state senator from California; and Miguel, Richard's much younger, mustachioed companion of Cuban descent. Georgie noticed immediately that no one spoke directly to her or Miguel.

They think I don't have anything worth saying, she thought. She turned the napkin over and over in her hands, as if wringing it out.

Before Joe, she'd never been around people with money. Back home, money was the local doctor or dentist, someone who could afford to send a child to private school.

Hannah, dressed in a simple black uniform, brought out fish chowder and stuffed lobster tail. The guests smoked between courses. Occasionally, Joe got up and made the rounds with the wine, topping off the long-stemmed crystal glasses she'd imported from France. After the entrées had been served, Hannah set rounds of roasted pineapple in front of each guest.

"How many people live here?" Clark asked Joe, mouth open, juice running down his chin.

"About two hundred and fifty," she said, leaning back in her chair, an imperial grin on her face. "But they're always reproducing, no matter how many condoms I hand out. There's one due to give birth any day now. What's her name, Hannah?"

"Celia."

"Will she go to the hospital?" Clark asked.

"I run a free clinic," Joe said.

"You have a doctor here?"

"I'm the doctor," Joe said, grinning. "I'm the doctor and the king and the sheriff. I'm the factory boss, the mechanic too. I'm the everything here. I give out mosquito nets and I sell rum. I sell more rum than anything."

"Well, more rum then!" Clark said, laughing.

Joe stood up, grabbed an etched decanter full of amber-colored liquor, unscrewed the top, and took a swig. She passed it down the table, and everyone but the financiers' wives did the same. Georgie kept her eyes on Marlene, who seemed unimpressed, distracted. She removed a compact mirror from her bag and ran her pointer finger along her forehead, as if rubbing out the faint wrinkles.

When she wasn't speaking, Marlene let her cigarette dangle out of one side of her mouth, or held it with her hand at her forehead, resting on her wrist as if she was tired of the world. She smoked Lucky Strikes, Joe said, because the company sent them to her by the cartonful for free.

"How does she do it?" Georgie whispered to Joe, hoping for a laugh. "How does her cigarette never go out?"

Joe ignored her, leaning instead to Marlene. "Tell me about your next film," she said, drumming her fingers on the white tablecloth.

"We'll start filming in the Soviet Occupation Zone," Marlene said, exhaling.

"No Western?"

"Soon. You like girls with guns, don't you, Joe?"

"And your part?" Joe asked.

"A cabaret girl," Marlene said. "But the cold-hearted kind. My character is a Nazi collaborator."

Joe raised her eyebrows.

"Despicable," Marlene said in her husky voice, "isn't it? Compelling, though, I promise."

"You always are," Joe said.

Georgie sighed and stabbed a piece of pineapple with her fork. The rum came to Marlene and she turned the bottle up with one manicured hand. She even knew how to drink beautifully, Georgie thought.

Joe moved her fingers to Georgie's thigh and squeezed. It was almost a fatherly gesture, Georgie felt. A we-will-talk-about-this-later gesture. When the last sip of rum came to Georgie, she finished it off, coughing a little as the liquor burned her throat.

"More rum?" Joe asked the table, glancing at the empty decanter.

"Champagne if you have it," Marlene said.

"Of course," Joe said. She pushed her chair back and went to discuss the order with a servant in the kitchen.

Georgie shifted uncomfortably in her chair, anxious at the thought of being left alone with Marlene. Next to her she could see Miguel stroking the senator's hand underneath the table while the senator carried on a conversation about the war with the financiers.

"And you," Marlene said to Georgie. "Do you plan on returning to Florida soon? Pick up where you left off with that mermaid act?"

Georgie felt herself blushing even though

she willed her body not to betray her.

"It's no picture show," Georgie said, smiling sweetly. "But I suppose I'll go back one of these days."

"I suppose you will," Marlene said, staring hard at her for a minute. Then she flicked the ashes from her cigarette onto the side of her saucer and stood up, her plate of food untouched. Georgie watched her walk across the room. Marlene had a confident walk, her hips thrust forward and her shoulders held back as if she knew everyone was watching, and from what Georgie could tell, scanning the table, they were.

Marlene slipped into the kitchen. Georgie imagined her arms around Joe, a bottle of champagne on the counter. Bedroom eyes.

Georgie took what was left in Joe's wineglass and decided to get drunk, very drunk. The stem of the glass felt like something she could break, and the chardonnay tasted like vinegar in her mouth.

When Joe and Marlene didn't return after a half hour, Georgie excused herself, embarrassed. She climbed the long staircase to her room, took off her dress, and stood on the balcony, the hot air on her skin, watching the dark ocean meet the night sky, listening to the water crash gently onto the island.

Some days it scared her to be on the small island. When storms blew in you could watch them approaching for miles, and when they came down it felt as if the ocean could wash right over Whale Cay.

I could always leave, Georgie thought. I could always go back home when I've had enough, and maybe I've had enough.

She sat down at Joe's desk, an antique secretary still full of pencils and rubber bands Joe had collected as a child, and began to write a letter home. Then she realized she had nothing to say.

She pictured her house, a small, white-sided square her father had built with the help of his brothers within walking distance of the natural springs. Alligators often sunned themselves on the lawn or found the shade of her mother's forsythia. Down the road there were boys running glass-bottom boats in the springs and girls with frosted hair and bronzed legs just waiting to be discovered or, if that didn't work, married.

And could she go back to it now? Georgie wondered. The bucktoothed boys pressing their faces up against the aquarium glass to get a better look at her legs and breasts? The harsh plastic of the fake mermaid tail? Her mother's biscuits and her father's old car and egg salad on Sundays?

She knew she couldn't stay at Whale Cay forever. But she sure as hell didn't want to go home.

In the early hours of morning, just as the sun was casting an orange wedge of light across the water, Joe climbed into bed, reeking of alcohol and cigarette smoke. She put her arms around Georgie and whispered, "I'm sorry."

Georgie didn't answer, and although she hadn't planned on responding, began to cry, with Joe's rough arms across her heaving chest. They fell asleep.

She dreamed of Sarasota.

There was the cinder-block changing room that smelled of bleach and brine. On the door hung a gold star, as if to suggest that the showgirls could claim such status. A bucket of lipsticks sat on the counter, soon to be whisked away to the refrigerator to keep them from melting.

Georgie pulled on her mermaid tail and slipped into the tank, letting herself fall through the brackish water, down, down to the performance arena. She smiled through the green, salty water and pretended to take a sip of Coca-Cola as customers pressed their noses to the glass walls of the tank. She flipped her rubber fish tail and sucked air from a plastic hose as elegantly as she could, filling her lungs with oxygen until they hurt. A few minnows flitted by, glinting in the hot Florida sun that hung over the water, warming the show tank like a pot of soup.

Letting the hose drift for just a moment, Georgie executed a series of graceful flips, arching her taut swimmer's body until it made a circle. She could see the audience clapping and decided she had enough air to flip again. Breathing through the tricks was hard, but a few months into the season, muscle memory took over.

Next Georgie pretended to brush her long blond hair underwater while one of Sarasota's many church groups looked on, licking cones of vanilla ice cream, pointing at her.

How does she use the bathroom? Can she walk in that thing? Hey, sunshine, can I get your number?

The next afternoon, as the sun crested in the cloudless sky, Marlene, Georgie, and Joe had lunch on Femme Beach. Marlene wore an enormous hat and sunglasses and reclined, topless, in a chair. She pushed aside her plate of blackened fish. Joe, after eating her share and some of Marlene's, kicked off her shoes and joined Georgie in the water, dampening her khaki shorts. Neither of them spoke for a moment.

"Marlene needs a place where she can be herself," Joe said eventually. "She needs one person she can count on, and I'm that person."

"Oh," Georgie said, placing a palm on top of the calm water. "Is it hard being a movie star?"

Joe sighed. "She's been out pushing war bonds, and she's exhausted. She's more delicate than she looks. She drinks too much."

"You're worried?"

"Sometimes she's not allowed to eat. It's hard on her nerves."

"Is this why the other girls left?" Georgie asked, looking out onto the long stretch of water. "You could have mentioned her, you know. You could have told me."

"Try to be open-minded, darling."

"I'll try," Georgie said, diving into the water, swimming out as far as she ever had, leaving Joe standing knee-deep behind her. Maybe Joe would worry, she thought, but when she looked back, Joe was in a chair, one hand on Marlene's arm, and their heads were tipped toward each other, oblivious to anything else.

What exhausted Georgie about Joe's guests was that they were all-important. And important people made you feel not normal, but unimportant.

That night the other guests went on a dinner cruise on the *Mise-en-scène,* while Joe entertained Marlene, Georgie, and Phillip. They were seated at a small table on one of the mansion's many balconies, candles and torches flickering, bugs biting the backs of their necks, wineglasses filled and refilled.

"How do you like Whale Cay?" Phillip asked Marlene.

"I prefer the drag balls in Berlin," she said, in a voice that belied her boredom. "But you know I've been coming here longer than you've been around?"

Marlene leaned over her bowl of steamed mussels, inspecting the plate. She pushed them around in the broth with her fork. "Tell me how you got to the island?" she asked Phillip, who, to Georgie, always seemed to be sweating and had a knack for showing up when Joe had her best liquor out.

"After Yale Divinity School —"

"He sailed up drunk in a dugout canoe. I

threatened to kill him," Joe interrupted.
"Then I built him his own church," she said
proudly, pointing to a small stone temple
perched on a cliff, just visible through the
brush. It had two rustic windows with
pointed arches, almost Gothic, as if it
belonged to another century.

"He sleeps in there," Joe said.

"I talk to God," Phillip said, indignant,
spectacles sliding down his nose. He slurped
his wine.

"Is that what you call it?" Joe said, rolling
her eyes.

"What do you have to say about all this?"
Marlene asked Georgie.

"About what?"

"God."

"Why would you ask me?" Georgie felt
her face get hot.

"Why not?"

Georgie remembered the way sitting in
church made her feel pretty, her mother's
hand over hers. She could recall the smell
of her mother, the same two dresses she
wore to church, her thrifty beauty and dime-
store lipstick and rough hands and slow
speech and way of life that women like Joe
and Marlene didn't know. Despite Phillip,
the church at Whale Cay still had holiness,
she thought. Just last week Hannah had

sung "His Eye Is on the Sparrow" after Phillip's sermon, and it had brought tears to Georgie's eyes, and taken her to a place beyond where she used to go in her hometown church, something past God as she understood Him, something attainable only when living away from everyone and everything she had ever known. Even if He wasn't a certain thing, He could be a feeling, and maybe she'd felt Him here. That day she'd realized she was happier on Whale Cay than she'd ever been anywhere else. She'd been waiting all her life for something big to happen, and maybe Joe was it.

"I suppose I don't know anything about God," she said. "Nothing I can put into words."

"You aren't old enough to know much yet, are you? You haven't been pushed to your limits. And you, Joe?" Marlene asked. "What do you know?"

Joe was quiet. She shook her head, coughed.

"I guess I had what you'd call a crisis of faith," she said. "When I drove an ambulance during the First War. I saw things there I didn't know were possible. I saw —"

Marlene cupped her hand over Joe's. "Exactly," she said. "Those of us who have witnessed the war firsthand — how can you feel another way? We've seen the godless landscape."

Firsthand, Georgie thought. What was firsthand about seeing a war from a posh hotel room with security detail, cooing to soldiers from a stage? Firsthand was her brother Hank, sixteen months dead, who'd been found malnourished and shot on the beach in Tarawa.

"That's exactly when you need to let Him in," Phillip said, glassy-eyed.

"You have a convenient type of righteousness," Joe said.

"Perhaps."

"I don't see how a priest can lack commitment in these times," Marlene said, scratching the back of her neck, eyes flashing.

Phillip rose, flustered. "If you'll excuse me, one of our native women is in labor," he said, "and I must attend." He turned to Joe. "Celia's been going for hours now."

"Her body knows what to do," Joe said, lighting a cigarette.

Joe and Marlene smoked. Georgie poured herself another glass of wine, finding the silence excruciating. Nearby a peahen screamed from a roost in one of the small trees that flanked the balcony. The island had been a bird sanctuary before Joe bought it, and exotic birds still fished from the shore.

"Grab a sweater," Joe instructed, standing up, stamping out her cigarette. "I want to take you girls racing."

The water was shiny and black as Joe pulled Marlene and Georgie onto a small boat shaped like a torpedo. It sat low on the water and had room for only two, but Georgie and Marlene were thin and the three women pressed together across the leather bench seat.

"Leave your drinks on the dock," Joe warned. "It's not that kind of joyride."

Not five minutes later they were ripping through the water, Georgie's hair blown straight back, spit flying from her mouth, her blue eyes watering. At first she was petrified. She felt as if the wind was exploring her body, inflating the fabric of her dress, tunneling through her nostrils, throat, and chest. A small sound escaped her mouth but was thrown backward, lost, muted. She looked down and saw Marlene's jaw set into a tight line, her knuckles white as her long fingers gripped the edge of the seat. Joe pressed on, speeding through the blackness until it looked like nothingness, and Georgie's fear became a rush.

The bottom of the boat slapped the water,

skipped over it, cut through it, and it felt as though it might capsize, flip over, skid across the surface, dumping them, breaking their bodies. Georgie's teeth began to hurt and she bit her tongue by mistake. The taste of blood filled her mouth but she felt nothing but bliss, jarred into another state of being, of forgetting, a kind of high.

"Enough," Marlene yelled, grabbing Joe's shoulder. "Enough! Stop."

"Keep going," Georgie yelled. "Don't stop."

Joe laughed and slowed the boat, cutting the engine until there was silence, only the liquid sound of the water lapping against the side of the craft.

"Take me back to the shore," Marlene snapped.

Georgie stood up, nearly losing her balance.

"What are you doing?" Joe demanded.

"Going for a swim," Georgie said.

Georgie kicked off her sandals, unbuttoned her sundress, leaving it in a pool on the deck of the boat. She dove into the black water, felt her body cut through it like a missile.

"We're a mile offshore! Get back in the boat!" Joe shouted.

Joe cranked the engine and circled, looking for Georgie, but everything was dark and Georgie stayed still so as not to be found, swimming underwater, splashless.

"Leave me," she yelled out. "I'm fine."

"You're being absurd. This is childish!"

Eventually, after Marlene's repeated urging, Joe gave up and headed for shore.

Georgie oriented herself, looking up occasionally at the faint lights on the island, the only thing that kept her from swimming out into the open sea. It felt good to scare Joe. To do what she wanted to do. To scare herself. To do the one thing she was good at, to dull all of her thoughts with the mechanics of swimming, the motion of kicking her feet, rotating her arms, cutting through the water, dipping her face into the warm sea and coming up for air, exerting herself, exhausting her body, giving everything over to heart, blood, muscle, bone.

That night, Georgie crept into the bedroom, feeling a little less helpless than she had the night before. The bed was empty, as she expected it might be. Even if Joe was with Marlene, she would still be worried, and Georgie liked the idea of keeping Joe up at night.

She went to the bathroom to comb her hair before bed. She stared at herself in the mirror. The overhead light was too bright. Her eyes looked hollow. She should eat more, drink less, she thought. As she reached for the comb she heard whimpering in the walk-in closet. Her heart began to beat quickly. She tiptoed to the closet and opened the door to find Joe sitting with her back against the wall, silk blouse soaked in sweat, a cache of guns and knives at her feet. She was breathing rapidly, chest heaving. She looked up at Georgie with glistening, scared brown eyes.

"Go away," she said, her voice hoarse. "Don't look at me like this."

Georgie stood in the doorway, tan legs peeking out from underneath the white cotton gauze gown Joe had bought for her, unsure of what to say. "Are you okay?" she asked. "Are you sick?"

"I said go away."

But Georgie sensed hesitation in Joe's voice and kneeled down beside her, sliding two guns away, bringing Joe to her chest. Joe gave in, sweating and sobbing against Georgie's skin.

"You can't begin to understand what I saw," Joe whispered. "There were bombs whistling overhead, dropping in front of me as I drove. There were men without heads, arms without bodies, the smell of gangrene we had to wash from the ambulance — every day, that smell. There were the boys who died. I heard them dying. Their faces were burned off. They were not human anymore. I can still see them."

"Shh," Georgie said. "That was a long time ago and you're here now. You're safe."

"Why did you leave me like that?"

"I just wanted to swim."

"I thought you were dead."

"Where's Marlene?"

"Asleep. In the stone house."

Georgie kissed Joe tenderly on the forehead, cheeks, and finally her mouth, and eventually they moved to the bed. Georgie had never been the aggressor, but she pushed Joe onto her back and pinned her wrists down, straddling her, biting her neck and shoulders.

That night, as they lay quietly on the bed, they could hear the faint sounds of a woman screaming, not in anger but in pain. Celia, Georgie thought, wincing.

When morning came, Joe acted as if nothing had happened, and Georgie found her standing naked on the patio, newsboy cap over her short hair, her toned and broad body sunned and confident, big white American teeth clenching a cigar from which she never inhaled.

"Shall we have breakfast with Marlene?" Joe said.

"I thought —"

"Don't think. Don't ever make the mistake of thinking here."

That night Georgie came to the dinner table with a renewed sense of entitlement. She belonged there. She sat down, considered her posture, and took a long drink of white wine, peering at the guests over the rim of her glass.

Marlene charged into the dining room like a bull. She plowed past the rest of the company, ignored Georgie, and reached for Joe's hand across the table.

Hannah set a shrimp cocktail and sliced lemons in front of each guest.

Phillip and Joe were in an argument about using the boat to take Celia to the hospital in Nassau.

"Just put her on the goddamned boat," Phillip said, ignoring his food. "She's been in labor for two days."

"What did they do before I was here?" Joe asked, exasperated, letting her fork hit the plate in disgust. "Tell her to just do that."

"Darling, have another glass of wine," Marlene said. "Don't get worked up."

"Have you seen her?" Phillip demanded.

"Have you *heard* her? She's suffering. She's dying. What don't you understand?"

"I've seen suffering," Joe said. "Real suffering."

"Oh don't pull out your old war stories now," Phillip scoffed, tossing his greasy, unwashed hair to the side.

"Joe —" Georgie began.

"It's not your place," Marlene said. "This is Joe's island."

"Just get the boat and let's go," Phillip interrupted. "Let's go now. She's going to die. I'm going to get a stretcher and we'll put her on the boat."

"You'll do what I tell you to do," Joe snapped, solemn and intimidating. "For starters, you can shower and sober up before you come to my dinner table." Georgie looked down at her plate, at once ashamed of Joe's savage authority and in awe of it.

"Do you want to go outside with me?" she whispered, lightly touching Joe's shoulder. "Walk this off, think about it?"

Joe ignored her.

Phillip stood up from the table, foggy spectacles sliding off his nose in the wet heat. "Sober up? Please. You're so regal, aren't you? The villagers hate you. You punish them for infidelity and you've got a dif-

76

ferent woman here every month. You walk around with a machete strapped to your chest like you're just waiting for an uprising. Maybe you'll get what you want," he said. "They're talking about it, you know. Maybe we'll just take the boat."

Joe stood up and leered at Phillip, practically spitting across the table. "They can hate me all they want; they need me. Why don't you get back on that goddamned canoe you came in on? Yale degree my ass. You're a deserter. Don't think I don't know it."

"You don't know anything about me," Phillip shot back, storming out of the dining room. Georgie could hear him shouting as he marched away in the still air. "Blessed is the one who does not walk in step with the wicked!"

"I think we should take her to Nassau," Georgie said, turning to Joe.

"What do you know?" Marlene snapped.

"It's the right thing to do."

"A little rum will make us all feel better," Joe said, forcing a smile. "Hannah?"

"It doesn't make *me* feel better at all," Georgie said quietly. She had been determined to hold her own tonight, to look Marlene in the eye, to prove to her that she was a worthy partner for Joe. But she quickly sensed a loss of control, of confidence.

"It's all about you, is it?" Marlene asked. "You're lucky to be here, darling, you know that?"

"We need to get the hell out of this room," Joe announced, knocking over her chair as she stood up.

Joe gathered her guests in the living room, which was full of plush sofas and polished tables covered in crystal ashtrays. Mounted swordfish and a cheetah skin decorated the whitewashed walls.

Joe put on a Les Brown record and opened a cigar box. She clamped down on a cigar and carried around a decanter of scotch, topping off her guests' drinks.

"No restraint," she said. "Drink as much as you want. It's early."

Georgie leaned against a window, gulped down her drink, and stared out at the black sea. Joe pulled her away and into a corner.

"Are you having a good enough time?" she asked. "Are you angry?"

"What do you think?" Georgie said.

"You're drunk," Joe said.

"What?" Georgie asked, voice falsely sweet. "I'm the only one who's not allowed to have a big night?"

"It's just unusual for you," Joe said.

"We should take the boat to Nassau," Georgie said.

"You're slurring," Joe said. "And besides, I've said no. If I go now, I'll lose my authority."

"You might lose it anyway."

Joe was silent and turned to refresh her drink, pausing to talk with the financiers. Georgie stayed at the window. She could hear the islanders' voices outside. She couldn't understand what they were saying, but they were loud and animated. Hannah, who was making the rounds with a box of cigars, lingered by the window, a worried expression on her face.

Would the native islanders riot? Maybe. But what weighed most heavily on Georgie was the sense of being complicit in Celia's suffering.

Marlene approached, locking eyes with her. She topped off Georgie's glass and lit another cigarette.

"Got ugly in there, didn't it?" she said, exhaling.

Georgie nodded.

"Bet you don't see that every day in the mermaid tank," Marlene said. "But Joe can handle it. Even if you can't. Those of us that have been to the war —"

Georgie held up a hand, stopping Marlene. She felt claustrophobic, drunk. She knew she wasn't thinking clearly. Her body was warm from the rum and wine and she felt anxious, like she needed to move.

"Tell Joe I'm off for a walk. To think about things."

"Stay out awhile," Marlene said, calling after her.

Georgie left the house through the kitchen and walked away from the group of islanders who had clustered near the dock. She wanted to tell them that they were right, that they should take the boat, but she was too ashamed to look them in the eyes, too afraid to speak against Joe. She wanted to talk to Phillip, so she followed the path of crushed oysters and sand north toward the simple silhouette of the small stone church.

Georgie recalled the hymn her mother liked — "O God, Our Help in Ages Past," and couldn't keep herself from singing. Her tongue felt too big for her mouth, but still the words filled her with unexpected serenity. She took another drink from the crystal tumbler she'd carried from the house and sang the first verse again, and then again, until she could feel her mother's nails on her back, calming her, loving her to sleep.

She found Phillip passed out on a wooden bench in front of the church.

"Phillip," she said, gently rocking him with her hands. He was shirtless and his skin was warm. A single silver cross Joe had given him hung around his neck.

"Phillip," she said. He stirred but didn't open his eyes. She pinched the skin above his hip bone.

"What?" he said, opening his eyes into slits.

"Take the boat. Just take it."

"I'm in no shape to drive a boat."

"You have to. Someone has to."

"I like you, Georgie," Phillip said. "But you need to leave me the hell alone now." He waved her off with one hand, the other tucked underneath his head.

"But you said —"

"I give up. You should too." He rolled away from her, turning his face toward the back of the bench.

She took another sip of her drink while waiting for him to roll back over. When he didn't she walked to the place where the sand broke off into high cliffs, and began to pace the rim of the island, staring at the water below.

Looking down at the waves from the cliffs, she remembered Florida. She remembered sipping on the air hose and drinking Coca-Cola while tourists watched her through thick glass at the aquarium show. Sometimes Georgie had to remind herself that she could not, in fact, breathe underwater.

"Whatever you do," the aquarium owner had said, "be pretty."

And so the girls always pointed their toes and ignored the charley horses in their calves, or the way their eyes began to sting in the salt water. Georgie recalled the feeling of her hands on the arch of another swimmer's back as they performed an underwater adagio, the fatigue in her body after the back-to-back Fourth of July shows. She remembered a time when she felt good about herself.

She thought of Joe, and her arm around Marlene's back. She thought of the stone house, and for a minute, she wanted to leave Whale Cay and return home. But home would never be the same.

In a few days the yacht would pull away and Joe would wake her up with coffee in bed. Hannah would make her eggs, runny and heaped on a slice of white toast with fruit on the side. She would take her morning swims and read a book underneath the shade of a palm. And would that be enough?

They had a rock in the yard back home. Her father used to lift the copperheads out of the garden shed with his hoe and slice them open with the metal edge, their poisonous bodies writhing without heads for a moment on top of the rock. The spring ritual had horrified and intrigued Georgie, and it was what she pictured now, standing above the sea, swaying, the feeling of rocks underneath her feet.

But she might never see that rock again, she thought.

It was dark and she couldn't see well. There was shouting in the distance. She felt bewildered, restless.

She set down her glass and took off her sandals. She would feel better in the water, stronger.

With casual elegance, she brought her hands in front of her body and over her head and dove off the cliff. As she approached the water, falling beautifully, toes pointed, she wondered if she'd gotten mixed up and picked the wrong place to dive.

She was falling into the tank again, the brackish water in her eyes, but no one was watching.

She was cherry pie.

She was a ticker tape parade.

Her hands hit the water first. The water rushed over her ears, deafening her. Her limbs went numb, adrenaline moving through her until she was upright again, gulping air.

She treaded water, fingers moving against the dark sea, pushing it away to keep herself afloat. There were rocks jutting out from the water, a near miss. There were strange birds nesting in the tall grass, a native woman bleeding on a straw mattress in a hut on the south shore, a stone house strangled by fig trees.

*Norma Millay's high school gradua-
tion photo. Camden, Maine, 1912.*

**Photo reprinted with permission of the
Camden Public Library.**

Norma Millay's Film Noir Period

ACT I

Her earliest memory is a fever dream, her mother, Cora, retreating from her bedside, a backlit head surrounded by a pale yellow aura. *Sailing, sailing over the bounding main,* Cora sings, still in her nurse's uniform with the puffed sleeves and starched collar. *Where many a stormy wind shall blow.* Her voice fades into silence. Diminuendo, thinks Norma, who longs to bring Cora's voice back, to wrap herself in the familiar mezzo-soprano until she falls asleep, but now she's left clinging to a thread of consciousness.

Sometimes Cora sets the metronome on top of the old piano, adamant the girls should learn time signatures. "You don't have the luxury of being mediocre," she says, leaning over them with a humorless face. "Not moderato, allegro!" In the recesses of her mind Norma can hear the tick-tick-ticking increasing in speed until it flatlines into a solid wall of sound. She nods off, wakes up, nods off again on the damp pillow.

The Maine winter is cold enough to freeze the soft curls on her head after a bath, and the water that leaks onto the kitchen floor, but tonight she sweats like it's a July afternoon on the bay. She keeps one leg on top of the pile of worn quilts. She thinks of eating pickled figs in early summer. Her eyes are hot and a briny taste fills her mouth.

Vincent and Kathleen share the bed, their downy knees and sharp elbows pushing at her back and legs, which she resents and cherishes all at once. The smell of their bodies, not so frequently bathed in winter, is familiar, something like lavender soap, sweat, and pine sap, which falls into their hair when they collect kindling for the stove. She loves knowing her sisters are by her side even as Cora leaves in the dark of morning with an ugly brown coat buttoned over her uniform. "You're a tribe," she told them years ago, on their first day back to school after typhoid fever, when she'd cut off their hair and they looked like pale, starving page boys in white dresses. "You stick together."

■ ■ ■ ■

Norma realizes there's work you talk about and work you don't. She pictures her mother bustling around a tubercular patient's bed, then cutting her own copper-colored hair at night and weaving it into the scalp of a doll. She imagines the rhythm of the needle as it pulses in and out of the muslin. Piercing, popping, pulling through.

"Teach us how," she and her sisters used to beg, kneeling at Cora's chair, rifling through her sewing basket and the pouches of human hair she collected from friends.

"I'll teach you to read and sing," she'd say, shaking her head. "But not to work with hair." The girls knew they were not to play with the doll; it would be sold for rent money.

Norma knows when they wake up they'll be alone in the dim kitchen, smearing day-old bread with measured dollops of blueberry jam, warmed on the stove. They'll do the washing until their fingers are numb with cold, sing songs their mother taught them, tell stories in bed about imaginary lovers —

what does a lover do so much as kiss? — while the modest fire becomes nothing but smoldering coals. They're a houseful of skinny girls, dirt-poor ingenues singing arias from a cabin in the swampy part of town near the mill, a place the shipbuilders have fled. The young forest is beginning to grow again, but lately it's bare enough to see the lean deer moving through.

In the morning, Norma, too ill to eat, stares out of the window onto the Megunticook River, its edges frozen and tinged with crimson dye from the mills. Snow and ice form a diamond-like crust over the window-panes, illuminated by pale rays of sunshine, so she peers out at the river through a clear spot on the window, her breath fogging up the sparkling glass.

The rose hips outside the window are black; months before, when they were plump and orange, she used to chew them. Poor girl's candy.

Vincent is nearby, one small foot folded underneath her body as she mends Cora's blouse. Her lips are moving and Norma wonders if she's reciting or composing; it's as if she's already gone from them. "We must save for Vincent's sake," Cora says. "We must try for a scholarship, subscribe to poetry magazines."

Though Norma and Kathleen both write poetry, sing, and act, only Vincent gets letters in the mail, letters full of praise and promise. It is, Norma thinks, as if only one of us can get out of this cold house, and it's going to be Vincent.

Very well and good, she thinks, trying to be just in her wants and needs. All is as it should be.

There are things to look forward to, though, she tells herself. Boats on the bay in summer, reading on the rocks, picnics among the ferns on Mount Battie.

She begins to shake. Her teeth chatter; in her head it's the sound of ceramic plates falling against each other in the sink.

"Come sit by me, Hunk," Vincent says, beckoning Norma to her chair. "It's cold by the window and you're dreadfully sick."

Norma curls next to her sister in the chair, as she often does, wriggling one arm behind

Vincent's back and laying a cheek on her bony shoulder. When she breathes in, her sister's claret-colored hair falls across her face, and she feels deep love tinged with resentment, like the pure ice leaching red dye from the river.

ACT II

Norma's thick hair is cut to her chin and she wears her secondhand fur coat with pomp, turning the collar up so it brushes against her wide but handsome jawline. While her sister's beauty is elfin and ethereal, Norma's is sumptuous, hardy, fervent. Vincent may be the genius, Norma thinks, but *I* am the femme fatale.

Vincent calls her Old Blond Plumblossom. They're stalking across MacDougal Street in worn heels, a block from the theater where they both work, hashing out a three-part harmony for the stage. Norma relishes the rush of mingling with so many people in the city. The way she can dance until midnight or give all her energy to rehearsals that last until daybreak, with Eugen and Jig staggering around and fighting, the women drinking and stitching costumes, legs dangling over the small stage.

"Charlie lost his temper last night," Norma says, interrupting Vincent's singing. "He doesn't like Ida being cast —"

"Dear Charlie is always losing his temper," Vincent says, sighing, slight affectation in her voice, picked up from her years at Vassar. "He hardly has one to keep."

"He thinks you'd make a better lead."

"He's right, of course," Vincent says, shrugging her shoulders. "And I appreciate his loyalty. I know he keeps it up to flatter you. But I'm plenty busy writing my *Aria.* Speaking of — Hold your C for me at the end of that first line."

Norma does as told, then Vincent hits a complementary note. They're supposed to be Furies or, as Vincent says, the Erinyes, and her idea is to make otherworldly sounds. "We're brutal avengers," she reminds Norma. "The melody should be haunting and rise to a sort of onslaught. I want beautiful but frenzied."

■ ■ ■ ■

"Try G," Norma says, gently correcting her sister. "Like this."

"And E major for Mum," Vincent says, unleashing a note that becomes a cloud of breath in the air.

"Mum will have to be offstage left," Norma says, thinking of Cora's tendency to jockey for a role onstage. She looks up at the wan sky, then into the golden insides of a café with a green awning. She imagines a steaming hot cup of coffee and a pastry, but there's no money for pastries, just a big lunch at Polly Holladay's.

Her pace, and then Vincent's, quickens, probably because they're talking about Cora. She's the one topic capable of dividing them, and they both tend to get anxious when she comes up. Taking a longer stride causes the backs of Norma's shoes to rub against her heels and she winces. Vincent had called her to New York in a letter, saying, "We'll open our oysters together." But Cora had come too.

■ ■ ■ ■

"We can't just put Mum on the shelf," Vincent says, dodging a lamppost. "You know that."

Norma nods, though she's ready to be young and free in the city, and Vincent's extreme loyalty to their mother baffles her.

"We'll *all* be offstage," Vincent says. "Heard but not seen."

"Fine," Norma says, not wanting to fight.

At night, in their cramped apartment, Cora peers over her small spectacles and refuses to drift out of young conversation like most women her age. "I, too, slept around if it suited me," she announced one evening at dinner, a candlelit meal over a rickety table that included one of Vincent's literary suitors, a kind but unathletic man who couldn't hide his shock. "Why shouldn't my girls do the same?" Cora continued, nonchalant.

Norma was embarrassed, but not surprised, while Vincent laughed heartily and poured her mother another glass of wine.

Vincent is the sun they orbit now, not quite a mother figure but a revered one. One night, when they'd been drinking, she asked Norma to sweep the kitchen.

"I *always* clean the kitchen."

"Oh don't be revisionist. We all cleaned the kitchen growing up."

"Who do you think kept house when you went off to Vassar?"

"Tell me," Vincent said, pausing in the doorway, owning every inch of her five-foot frame. "What kind of ride is it, on my coattails? Is it good?"

In the morning, Vincent groveled, but Norma waved her off. We're all hustlers, she thought. I may have come into the theater on Vincent's coattails, but I've stayed because I'm damn good at what I do.

Norma has held a gun, silhouetted onstage, lights dark. She's been a mermaid, then a barmaid, in Djuna Barnes's *Kurzy of the Sea,* taken direction from Eugene O'Neill, when he's sober enough to give it. She's delivered a monologue in a subterranean city of the future in a costume shaped like a pyramid, a halo over her head dangling from a well-bent wire. She's been the highlight of a bad production, a critic writing, "Even Norma Millay's superb acting couldn't save this show . . ."

And Charlie — Charlie has seen her talent. Dear, grumpy Charlie, who acts but just wants to paint, even though in her heart of hearts she believes he isn't as talented as he thinks; are any of them? But that's part of his charm, the vulnerability packed alongside the swagger and hot temper.

If Charlie is busy tonight, or in a foul mood, or painting, she thinks, I'll go home and share a bed with Vince and Mum.

When she's standing on the stage it's easy to believe that she's nearly famous, that she has achieved something, but there are times, like during a half-empty matinee, when the gig feels insignificant. Groundbreaking or not, they are, after all, a troupe that began in a neglected fishing shack that smelled of rotted wood and dead cod.

Later that night, snow hurls itself against their barred window in the Village, while Norma covers her head with a pillow to drown out Cora's snoring and the sound of Vincent making love to a poet in the kitchen. "Renounce me," she can hear Vincent saying. "Renounce me."

ACT III

"Plumblossom, I *need* you to be brave," Vincent slurs. "Hurry the hell up!"

They're on the screened-in porch at Steeple-top, and Vincent is agitated and starting to loosen the waistband of her trousers. The flies hurl themselves at the lanterns; Vincent's farm doesn't have electricity and is surrounded by impenetrable darkness on nights when the moon is small. The sisters have eaten what feels like their weight in blueberries, swum naked in the pool made out of the stone barn foundation, and downed two bottles of wine. Vincent's husband, Eugen, is passed out on the couch inside, and she's thumping a syringe of morphine with expert hands.

■ ■ ■ ■

"I don't want to," Norma says, crushing her eyes shut. "This isn't good for you."

"You'll do it," Vincent says, exposing the white flesh of her backside. "Hunk, I *need* you to do it. Who cares how we raise the devil?"

Vincent has burned through more than one advance, clutches her stomach constantly, complains of her guts aching, and washes her meals down with gin, wine, anything. She still packs auditoriums for her readings, but if they could only see the track marks on her legs, Norma thinks.

"How can you turn your back on me?" Vincent says. "After everything I've done for you?"

"Just tell me how much," Norma says, sighing, throwing up her hands. "Though I feel like you're asking me to kill you."

"I'll die if you *don't* do it," Vincent says, "and that's the truth. I won't use caution. I'll plunge a syringe into both thighs."

■ ■ ■ ■

"You won't."

"Are you daring me?"

"Just use the damn syringe, Hunk."

"Write down the dose in the notebook," Vincent says, nodding to one on a glass table nearby.

Norma can see the lucidity in her eyes slipping away, but the imperial quality is still there. When Norma looks at the notebook she's horrified by the entries, morphine on the hour some nights. Vincent's cheeks already look flaccid, the whites of her eyes yellowed.

Perhaps Cora knows how bad things have gotten, but Cora is in Camden now, feeble and focused on her own writing, children's books and verses. And Kathleen is paranoid, and not to be trusted. No, this is my secret to keep with Eugen, she thinks, though anyone seeing Vincent now would know the truth.

■ ■ ■ ■

"Don't look at me with compassion," Vincent mumbles in a harsh, dry voice as she reclines on the divan she keeps out on the porch. "I don't want it."

Norma sits on the cool, hard floor and leans against the wicker base of the divan. Vincent reaches for her hand, and she gives it, and when she wakes in the early morning, her shoulder socket aches from reaching up for so long. In the early hours, when the sun is coming up and before the birds have started singing, Norma walks to the guest cottage and climbs in the single bed with Charlie, keeping the windows open. Startled by the roar of an engine, she wakes in time to see Eugen and Vincent speeding down the dirt road, top down, raccoon coats on to take the chill off the morning, her sister's hair raised by the wind.

They're going to town, perhaps, and it's understood that Norma should feed the dogs and horses. It is understood that she might pluck a tomato and eat it for dinner alongside some fresh eggs. It is understood that she should sense where she is needed and assist, and not drink the last of the wine.

ACT IV

A storm comes, and Norma must close up the big white barn across from the house. Her long white hair trails behind her as she runs across the damp grass in her yellow raincoat. The rain clouds her black, horn-rimmed glasses. A dark sedan is coming down the dirt road — no one comes down this road unless they're looking for her — Steepletop belongs to her now.

She enjoys having something people want. A smile plays at her lips, but she tamps it down. She leans against a maple tree on the edge of the road, presses her back against it, pulling one foot up on the trunk of the tree, flamingo-like. She lifts her chin and looks into the breeze so that it lifts her hair from her face.

I still know how to own a scene and cut a figure, she thinks.

The car slows, and a man rolls down the passenger-side window.

"Is this the Millay place?"

■ ■ ■ ■

"Perhaps," she says, coyly.

She walks toward the car and leans forward, one hand on her hip. She likes to think of herself as a hard-boiled heroine, and lets her eyes do the talking. The men are in their forties, thin and well-dressed.

"We were hoping to speak to someone about Mrs. Millay's papers," the man on the passenger side says politely. She can see his jacket draped across his knees.

"Of course you are."

"Can you help us?"

"I could. But I might not." She raises an eyebrow, which she keeps neat and plucked.

"We have Mrs. Millay's legacy in mind."

"You're one in a hundred, you know that? I see your type every month." She shakes her head.

"We won't trouble you long. We have a letter of introduction."

"You all do. Let me think about it. Come back in the morning."

"We just drove up for the day, and are headed back to the city —" The passenger seems desperate, and this delights Norma. This is what she has come to live for, reeling people in only to release them.

"Come back in the morning."

She turns her back to the idling car and heads up the steep hill to the farmhouse, where she pours herself a glass of red wine and scrambles an egg.

She likes to sleep alone in Vincent's bed, in Vincent's fine linen sheets with the too-long monogram, especially when the fall winds shake the apples from the trees and Charlie is chain smoking and painting nudes of another college student in his studio across the road. Was this how it was for Vincent on her last October night? Lonely? Too quiet? The hunters at work in the woods, a glass of wine in hand?

And what position is the college student in?

Norma wonders. Legs splayed open, draped in a red cloth, that same damn piece of red cloth he put over everyone? Does it matter?

She turns down the covers. She can reach the bureau from the bed and its contents, the book Vincent was reading the week she died, the rings she left in a ceramic dish. Norma slides her sister's rings over her arthritic fingers, on and off, on and off.

"How can you live like this?" Charlie has asked her.

She doesn't let him in Vincent's bed. She won't let him empty Vincent's yellowed mouthwash or move her suitcase. Squirrels have nested in the divan on the porch, and one made fast work out of books and a windowsill in the library. Cobalt-blue morphine bottles still glitter like sapphires in the trash pile. The kitchen ceiling is dotted with wet, circular spots of mold. But she doesn't want to change anything; adjusting a piece of sheet music on the piano, disturbing a ceramic deer on the kitchen shelf, moving the biting instructions Vincent left for the help, unfolding the towels in the bathroom — it might rob the place of her sister's spirit.

■ ■ ■ ■

Norma can't sleep well that night. It isn't that she hasn't seen Charlie, or that the tax bill has increased, or that the termites are nibbling away at the cottage. Something about the aspiring biographer worries her, or maybe it's the realization that she's now in her seventies and when she passes away someone *will* get the papers, someone will see the insides of Vincent's drawers. Though it's still dark outside, she pulls on pants, boots, and her yellow slicker and, armed with matches and a bag of Vincent's belongings, walks the quarter mile to the trash pile in the woods. She passes Cora's grave surrounded by an iron fence, and then the two heavy stones for Vincent and Eugen, surrounded by moss and fallen leaves.

I can't give away everything, she thinks. I'm not ready. *She's* not ready.

When Norma reaches the trash pile, she looks around to make sure she's alone. Young poets come out here, screwing each other desperately in the woods, carving their names into the trees, stealing glass bottles, hoping for magic to find them.

■ ■ ■ ■

Maybe it does.

Norma doesn't mind the poets. She lets them sleep in the cottage. She lets them sleep with Charlie too, and she's made love to more than one. She may be old, but they want to get close to Vincent and she's the best option they have.

Certain she's alone, she arranges kindling and starts a fire, onto which she tosses a handful of nude photographs, a few desperate-sounding letters, and Vincent's ivory dildo, which refuses to burn for a long time, but finally disappears into a dark, indeterminable object.

Chilled, she retraces her steps through the woods and returns to Vincent's bed, half-listening for the wheels of the dark sedan groaning over the gravel. Norma's silver hair is spread out across Vincent's pillow. It took her months to wash the linens after coming here. It took her months to find her appetite, to bring herself to look at the last poem Vincent wrote, the one that must have landed like a feather on the stairs next to her body after she fell.

She thinks of the catamounts slinking through the forest, the brown bear lumbering through the blueberry bushes in the early dawn. She knows how the farm is, and how it was, and that it is still a place where she can be alone with her sister.

On quiet mornings like this, Norma can most vividly picture Vincent in her blue robe, a little hunched, head surely aching, walking barefoot over the lawn with a notebook in hand, settling onto the ground, one small foot tucked underneath her body so that she could watch a fawn until the dew seeped into her nightgown, and the loyal doe returned.

We are what we can be, not what we ought to be.
— From Romaine Brooks's notebooks

ROMAINE REMAINS

On the third floor of her villa in Fiesole, Romaine tries to control the afternoon sun by slapping a yardstick against the blinds. A screaming wedge of white light falls across her face. Unable to rise from her chair, she rings for the houseboy, Mario.

He hears the clang of the bronze bell and sprints up from the kitchen, where he's been smoking cigarettes with the cook. He runs a hand through his thick hair and clears his throat before entering the room.

Signora, he says humbly, bowing his head.

Close the blinds, she says.

He nods solemnly and releases the wooden slats, which collapse against the window with a clatter. The wedge of light disappears. Romaine, he has learned, likes to sit alone in the dark.

He treads lightly across the floor. Noise, like motorbikes, or a woman singing one house over, can trigger Romaine's rage, and if he isn't careful she'll spend the afternoon bedridden with a pillow over her head, then complain about him to the night nurse, claiming, That boy exposes me to torture. She'll go on about how an artist must protect her senses, and no one likes her to go on about anything.

I will work today, she tells Mario, but when he returns with her canvas and paints, Romaine is asleep, body curled like a prawn, her head lolled to the side, large eyes closed, breathing heavily. She wears her usual outfit, a white silk blouse, loose bow tie, faded brocade jacket with dander on the shoulders. He hates the way gravity sucks at her chin, the crescent-shaped pillows of skin underneath her eyes. Her hair, occasionally dyed black, is short and unwashed, primarily because it is an act of great courage to wash her. The first time he tried, she slapped him with the washcloth.

You brute! The water is frigid, she complained, her body stiff in the cloudy tub, breasts drooping below the waterline. I'll die of cold.

She tells him to wake her if she sleeps during the day, that she does not like to sleep, that she has nightmares from childhood. But he never wakes her. One time he did and she accused him of touching her inappropriately.

You put your hands underneath my blouse, she said, snarling. Her right eye floated slightly away from the intended line of her gaze, as it always had.

Cristo! I would *never,* he exclaimed, backing away, his hands up in protest. His disgust was evident to Romaine and enraged her even more.

I'll have you arrested! she said, but her voice was hoarse and raspy and came out as a whisper. I was a beautiful woman, she said, lip curling. I had many lovers.

She's feeble but threatening, and he has to take her seriously; he needs this job, and she knows it. He made the mistake of telling her. No one ever works for Romaine longer than six months. She's too demanding, too proud, too suspicious. Last year she fired everyone and a nurse found her shivering in bed, weak from having not eaten for four days. What the nurse told him his first day of work: Romaine would rather die than compromise.

Mario tells his mother, who is eighty-six, that Romaine is ninety-three and has a closet full of silk opera capes. She doesn't wear glasses, he says.

She's paid for new eyes?

No, Mario says. She's more stubborn than

blindness itself.

Mario lives with his Spanish mother in a one-room flat in Fiesole; she had envisioned it as a paradise, but it did not feel this way. She takes on laundry and mending, and he often finds her hunched over the tub, swirling someone else's pants in the dull water. He'd grown up in Haro, Spain, and hoped to become a literature student, maybe a teacher, but his father died and his brothers were off working in the vineyards of Serralunga d'Alba. Someone had to stay home and care for Mama, even if she was tiresome, full of outdated gossip and complaints about the arthritis in her worn knuckles.

How did I come to spend all my time with two old women? Mario wonders, hating his life, hating his conscience for keeping him home when he'd been the studious one in the family. He'd stayed up many nights, chewing licorice and drinking weak coffee, poring over the old encyclopedias his aunt had given him. He was supposed to escape, not his brothers. He was supposed to fall in love, grab happiness by the throat.

I wish she would die, Mario thinks, looking at Romaine's limp body, the silver hairs on her upper lip, but he knows he'd have to go back to busing tables, bleaching napkins, cutting the mold off cheese rinds. Because

114

Romaine sleeps so much Mario can read books and Enzo, the cook, can drop acid and organize radical political meetings in the galley kitchen, drinking up Romaine's Barolos with his communist friends, thumping the ashes from his cigarette into her gnocchi.

Today her lunch, tomato soup and croquettes, is untouched on the tray, which she has pushed into the corner so as not to smell it. As far as he can tell, Romaine takes joy in nothing. She turns friends away, leaves letters unopened.

He tiptoes toward the door, hoping to get back to his novel, Caproni's translation of Céline's *Death on Credit*.

Mario!

She's awake. He sighs.

Can't you see that I'm doing my exercises?

Mi scusi.

She looks to the right, a hard right. Then to the left. She's exact in her movements; she's been doing these exercises daily for thirty years. Down, around, repeat. Now angles. Now close and far away.

Mario hears the neighbor's rottweiler barking. The dog sits on the rooftop patio across from Romaine's bedroom, howling at ambulances, barking for hours. Once the dog starts he can't quit.

115

You *must* make the dog stop, Romaine says, holding her trembling fingers to her temples.

Mario has tried explaining that he can't make the dog stop barking, but Romaine expects the impossible. So he opens the doors onto Romaine's terrace and yells at the thick-necked dog, who only barks harder and louder upon seeing Mario, frothing at the mouth, placing his front paws on the planters filled with red begonias. *Vaffanculo,* Mario mutters.

He picks up the broom they leave on the terrace and sweeps the dead blossoms from the terra-cotta tiles; as soon as the sun goes down Romaine will take her wine out here, as long as the dog is quiet. How can she be so paranoid when she can have anything she wants? he wonders.

When he comes inside Romaine is staring at the wall.

Should I set up your paints? he asks.

This question is a formality. Romaine has not painted in forty years.

Enzo is chopping a spoiled onion, wild-eyed as usual, shirt unbuttoned, glass of Barolo precariously placed on the marble chopping block. He has two bags of carrots nearby, which he will make into the juice that

Romaine drinks twice daily for her eyesight.

Ecco! he says, sweating, laughing, always laughing. *È la domestica!*

I'm a student.

You're a nurse! To an old woman with droopy tits and a mouth like a *marinaio*.

Zitto.

Do you have to wipe her ass? What's it like?

Mario ignores Enzo and collects the mail, opening the complex series of bolts Romaine has ordered installed on the door. Among her many paranoias: theft, blindness, and the belief that trees try to feed off one's "life force."

Romaine is not kind, but she is interesting; he will allow her that. Every week there's a letter from an art dealer in New York, hoping, no *begging,* for some of Romaine's work. She never responds.

An envelope stands out in today's stack: expensive lavender card stock, perfumed and embossed with a lily. He knows this stationery. It comes from Paris, from a woman named Natalie. He knows what will happen. He'll take these letters to Romaine on her dinner tray and she'll toss them on the floor or leave them underneath her silverware. Some days she painstakingly marks the envelope to be returned to sender:

117

"Miss Barney — Paris."

Mario usually reads the letters in the kitchen on his lunch break. Natalie's are his favorites; she seems to know she's having a one-sided conversation, that Romaine will never answer. She writes of the war, of the time twenty-odd years ago when she and Romaine were living in a Tuscan villa, gardening like peasants just to feed themselves. Her sentences move from hemorrhoid management to oral sex. Natalie is, from what he can tell, an elderly woman with an active libido.

Tonight, instead of taking the letter to Romaine, he puts it into his coat pocket and, after checking on his mother, reads it in bed, carefully unfolding the stationery. A lock of silver hair falls to the sheets. He scoops it up and places it on the bedside table.

I'm hungry for you. Old you, new you. Do you remember the ways we used to make love? And how often? Do you remember the way I used to reach inside your gown in the back room of a party? Do you remember the things we did under the table, my hand between your legs, the other wrapped around a glass of wine? And how people thought we were smiling at them, that our ecstatic faces were for them, but they never were . . .

The letter makes him feel — God, how does it make him feel?

As though there is vitality in the world, and he does not have it, he has never even tasted it in his mouth. He has never lived the way he wants to live, never felt in control, or able to express his desire for people and things. For men in new leather shoes drinking wine at the hotel bar, or the boys standing outside the less reputable *discotecas* smoking cigarettes. He has never been explicitly himself.

The next morning he makes his mother coffee and, with a newspaper over his head, runs to Villa Gaia to relieve the night nurse. Rain is rushing down the streets, clinging to the wisteria, washing over the empty Roman theater nestled into the hillside. Its circular steps have been there a thousand years and will be there a thousand more, he thinks. Everything is like that in this country. It rots, or it hardens and becomes an artifact, useless and revered.

He finds Romaine hunched over a steaming cup of tea in her bedroom, wearing a pair of green-tinted shades to protect her eyes. She removes them and looks him over. Mario notices that the ribbon to her blouse has come undone.

You're late.

Would you like me to fasten your bow? he asks, leaning in cautiously.

You've been sweating, she says, wrinkling her face. I can smell you.

He straightens up. I walk in the mornings, he begins. I didn't want to be late —

I'd like to go downstairs, she says, interrupting.

Mario nods, but inside he is furious, because getting her chair downstairs is an arduous task. Some days he asks Enzo to help, but lately Enzo has been too unkempt and boisterous, and Romaine would fire him on sight. Which, Mario is starting to think, might not be bad. With no cook he could read novels or take bread home to his mother, steal naps on the expensive sofa in the parlor. It's the only comfortable piece of furniture in the house. Everything else is so hard, so cold —

Marco!

Mario, he whispers.

Are you daydreaming? My chair!

Si, signora.

Twenty minutes later, his fingers and back ache and he's drenched in sweat, but they are on the second floor. She is silent. He wheels her down the hallway to see her paintings, realizing that all he wants is for her to say *Grazie, Mario. What would I do without you?*

He's seen her private gallery before, but it still makes his throat close up when the soft lights go on and the velvet curtains are lifted, because it is evidence that she possesses greatness. Or has the greatness gone away?

The canvases are enormous, and their frames are ornate. The paintings are dark: androgynous women in various brave poses or nude recline, their lithe bodies rendered in white, gray, and black. There's a woman in a cheetah-skin dress, another with trousers, a monocle, and a dachshund. A woman with a sallow complexion and eyes hidden by a top hat.

I painted this one in Paris, she says, nodding to a portrait of a woman in a fur stole with a commanding expression and the figurine of a black horse on the table in front of her.

Natalie, he thinks.

Paris must be beautiful, he says.

Je déteste Paris.

He's quiet for some time because he knows that's what she wants. He realizes that he's jealous of the life she's had, the money, the talent, the experiences. She calls herself American, but she's not American, he thinks, she is of the world, and how many people can say that?

I'd like you to leave now, she says.

I was sent to live with the maid, Romaine says when he brings her lunch, surprising him with conversation. My mother sent me away, abandoned me, left me to fend for myself, even though we were wealthy. I lived in squalor with a large family in an apartment that smelled of cabbage and spoiled butter.

Mario wonders if she is just talking, or actually talking to *him.*

Romaine pauses to choke down a stewed tomato. Then, she continues, I was sent off to boarding school. Mother didn't love me, you see, she never did. She loved my brother, St. Mar, and he was atrocious.

How so? Mario asks. He wants to engage her, be spoken to as an equal.

St. Mar was deficient, insane, violent, she says. You couldn't touch him. Not even to cut his hair, and it was long and tangled and he would grab the scissors and come at you. He was a boar that couldn't be brought out in public. When he was older his beard was long and he had sharp nails; he shuffled around the villa, moaning. Mother let him buy a monkey that bit children.

The women in my life were insufferable and strange, she continues, leaning back in her chair, the paleness of her face exacerbated by the maroon velvet upholstery. My sister, I'll have you know, had a child with my mother's boyfriend, and married him. This is before St. Mar died.

How did he die? Mario asks.

He starved himself. After he died Mother became convinced she could summon spirits. And when *she* died? I went from being an impoverished artist to owning six flats in Nice. She left me boxes of things, wigs and false teeth and the sense that I was haunted, always, by St. Mar's incessant crying, and Mother standing over me at night.

That sounds —

She comes to me still.

Mario nods.

I'm a martyr, she says, reaching gingerly for her teacup. I always have been.

The sound of her body trying to swallow the hot liquid is repugnant, but he feels some measure of pride that she's confiding in him. This is her way of saying that she knows he is more intelligent than the average *domestico,* that he has potential, that he's trustworthy.

Maybe she will see that I need help, he thinks, and send me off to Paris with a little annuity, deliver groceries to my mother.

I'm planning to move to Nice, you know, she says, removing her green glasses again, looking up with clear eyes. Your services will no longer be needed. You should make other plans.

Enzo, he says, wandering into the kitchen that evening, can you cover for me for a half hour? I need to check on Mama.

Certo, Enzo says, smiling at him with dark, wine-stained teeth. He's cleaning up the kitchen as if he's going to leave, but Mario knows he sleeps in the house so he doesn't have to pay rent elsewhere.

There is contempt between them, but that doesn't keep Mario from fantasizing about him. He imagines an angry, passionate tryst in the kitchen or the wine cellar. When he pictures these moments he has trouble looking Enzo in the eyes.

At home, Mario finds his mother sleeping on their couch. She's snoring loudly and her body is a fat little heap on the worn green upholstery. The small one-bedroom apartment with the concrete floor insults his taste. It's made for a rat, he thinks. I'm growing accustomed to nice materials.

He leaves his mother a baguette and a hunk of cheese and a note. He doesn't have the courage to tell her that soon he'll be out of a job.

When he returns to Villa Gaia, he hears shouting in the courtyard. Enzo has his shirt off and is swinging at a much larger man in a black T-shirt.

Lasciare! Mario hisses. You're going to wake Romaine and we'll all lose our jobs!

He owes me money, the large man mutters. I'm going to kill him.

Enzo, presumably drunk, swings again. The man ducks.

Kill him down the road, Mario says. *Prego.*

Heart pounding, Mario slinks into Villa Gaia, and silently creeps to Romaine's bedroom door to see if she's awake.

I hear you out there, she shouts. Come in at once.

Mario, head bowed, enters her dark bedroom. Romaine is propped on her pillows; a small light glimmers on her bedside table. The room is sparsely decorated, only a bed and bureau and the bedside table, but the wallpaper is hand-painted, a gray-blue background with white and silver cranes fishing in pools.

You've been sneaking around, haven't you?

No, signora, I —

You're fired. I can't sleep. I have called and called for you.

125

I'm sorry.

I'm ill. I'm ninety-three. I'm going blind. I can't walk.

Can I make you more comfortable?

Just leave, she barks, raising a spindly arm, pointing a skeletal finger at the door.

He backs out of the room and leans against the wall, heart racing still. If he loses this job now there'll be no rent money, no food.

The next morning, he brings her breakfast tray to the bedroom. Romaine sits up and rests against her pillows, grimacing, squinting at him. Her hair needs washing, he thinks.

Didn't I fire you last night? Didn't I tell you to leave?

No, signora. Mario smiles reassuringly at Romaine. You didn't. You must have had a bad dream. May I put cream in your coffee?

I never take cream!

May I open your windows?

Only a little.

The dry air comes in, and with it the scent of tiglio blossoms, a smell that seems too delicate and sweet for a woman like Romaine, who reaches for her glass of carrot juice.

I win, Mario thinks, smiling to himself as he backs through her bedroom door. Power is a funny thing. Sometimes you can just take it.

The next morning Romaine cracks one of her ancient teeth on biscotti. The misery in this world is constant, Romaine says, one liver-spotted hand to her temple.

I have suffered again and again, she continues.

Mario leaves and comes back with a cup of lemon tea.

He has dressed her in a soft, looping bow tie. Her head is tilted back, eyes suspicious. I didn't ask for that, she says, looking at the tea in front of her.

Tell me again about the flora and fauna of Capri, he says, kneeling at her side.

Why should I tell you anything? she asks, frowning down on him.

Because I'll listen.

Why don't I tell you about the woman who locked her children in a cage? I was a boarder in her house. They used to scream like animals. But I was always in bad places then, living in squalor. I had no money. I wanted to become a singer.

Would you sing for me?

Never.

Why did you stop?

The notes of song could never replicate

human suffering, she says, turning away from him. Not the way I could with line.

I want to see you draw, he says, casually brushing lint off her shoulder.

How dare you, she hisses, though he thinks maybe she is flattered. Perhaps the corner of her wry, bitter mouth has lifted for a second.

I don't believe you can do it anymore, he says, his voice teasing and almost, he realizes, malicious.

I can do it. I don't want to do it, but I *can* do it.

Do it, he says, thrusting a pen into her gnarled hand. He brings a sketchbook to her and scoots her up to the table.

No — my tooth is broken! Are you an imbecile?

Do it, he says, using the firmest voice he has ever used with her, with anyone.

I won't.

You will.

Looking up at him with confused, then furious eyes, she puts the tip of the pen to the paper. At first it does not move. She's just looking at it, or maybe she is looking within her mind. Her hand begins to slide across the dry paper, and a robed figure appears. She gives the figure wings and then draws two bald, stooped demons, which the

128

angel presses to her chest as if about to nurse them. Romaine doesn't pick up the pen; the line is constant and never-ending, sure of itself.

He sees her tongue — God, it is an ugly tongue — examining the jagged edge of the broken gray tooth as she looks at her work, letting the pen fall to the table. She grabs his arm and whispers: I'm in pain. Please call the dentist.

This is the price you have to pay, he thinks, looking down at her bulging eyes, for having a good life, for being able to wake up when you want, fuck who you want, travel the world and sleep in soft beds and never clean your own toilet. This is for your closet full of opera capes.

I'll see to it, signora, he says, pulling his arm from her cold grasp, gathering the drawing, leaving the room.

As he leaves, the rottweiler begins barking.

Marco! The dog, Romaine says.

He pretends he cannot hear her, and continues down the stairs.

Before he phones the dentist, he finds one of the letters from the art dealer, and places a call.

I have new work, he says, in a confident voice he can't believe is his own. And we're willing to sell.

On his next shift Mario finds Romaine sitting alone. She doesn't look up or acknowledge him. She isn't sleeping, but her body is in a state close to sleep, he thinks.

Romaine, he says, addressing her by name for the first time. She looks at him, confused. Overnight he has come up with a plan, and he's determined to put it into action, to claim the experiences that should have been his.

I have something to tell you, he says.

Don't waste my time, she mumbles, fingering the silk of her blouse, brushing the morning's crumbs from her lap.

She looks weaker, he thinks, pleased with the idea that she might become more vulnerable. That's what he wants. Vulnerable, but not dead. He takes a deep breath and continues.

The cook — you remember Enzo?

Of course I remember!

He's been using the galley kitchen as his private meeting space, Mario says — sighing as if this has bothered him morally — and there's been trouble. I broke up a fight the other night; I was worried they would wake you. Did they wake you?

I've told you that I rarely sleep. My

mother —

What would you like me to have done?

Fire him, of course, Romaine says, sighing, sagging into her chair.

Would you like to do it?

Take care of it, Romaine says, turning her large eyes to the window. I don't have the energy.

Mario goes first to the galley kitchen, which is hot and rank with spoiled vegetables and forgotten, decanted wine. A raw goose, head still intact, lies defeathered and gray on a platter, beak resting on its pimpled back. The unwashed butcher block is scarlet with blood, marred by years of haphazard cuts. Unable to find Enzo, Mario moves from room to room until he comes to Romaine's gallery. This is a sacred room, he thinks, and so when he finds Enzo sprawled in the corner, a sheet over his body, a white enamel pot of piss in the corner, he is furious, shaking with anger as he walks toward the sleeping cook and nudges him with the toe of his shoe, his father's shoe.

You've been let go, he says.

Enzo rubs his eyes, sits up, spits onto a corner of the sheet, and rakes it across his face. You're a big shot now? he says, blinking. How did you manage that?

If you don't believe me you can go and

131

speak with Romaine.

Fuck Romaine, he says, rising, standing nose to nose with Mario. Did you stick your tongue in her mouth?

Please don't make a scene, Mario says. He can smell Enzo's musky body odor and unwashed hair.

I'll take everything, Enzo shouts, getting angrier by the second. *Brutto figlio di puttana bastardo!*

Do what you think is right, Mario says, turning to leave. He's shaking inside, waiting for Enzo to strike him or throw something, but he doesn't. Mario calls the night nurse and tells her not to come, that Romaine has asked him to stay on for the night.

That evening, the house is quiet. Enzo has taken all the wine, and the cellar is barren. No matter, Mario thinks, running a finger along the shelves to clear the cobwebs. I'll order more. I can order anything. There are no limits.

Now he has absolute privacy and authority in the house. Romaine is asleep in her chair in the parlor; Mario enters her bedroom and walks straight to the closet, taking a silk opera cape from its hanger, sliding it over his own narrow shoulders, admiring himself in the Japanese mirror. He can't stop stroking the black silk. He wears the cape downstairs to clean the kitchen. He wears it to put out the trash. When the rottweiler begins to bark, he is so bold as to walk past Romaine wearing her own clothes, the fine clothes of her youth, and onto the patio, where, beneath a purple sky, he pelts the barking dog with Romaine's uneaten dinner, undercooked goose thighs and roasted potatoes. His fingers are greasy from handling the food, but he continues stroking the opera cape. The streets of Fiesole are quiet. The families are eating their late dinners in their fine homes, congratulating themselves, he thinks.

He wears her cape as he runs downstairs to the gallery, silk trailing behind him. He opens the door, not hesitating this time, and stands in front of Romaine's sad, beautiful paintings, imagining that they are his, that he is capable of such fine work. He wonders if it comes out of her naturally or how hard she had to work to master the shape of a face, the arc of human hands, the color of flesh. He doesn't want to imagine her working hard at anything, but it's worse to imagine her so fortunate as to have been born rich and egregiously talented as well. How miserably unfair.

The next night, after leaving Romaine to

fall asleep again in her chair, he puts on her delicate, pale pink pajama set, so pristine he's sure she's never worn it. The silk feels incredible against his skin, nearly liquid. He brushes his hair at her vanity using her brush. He buffs his nails. He sprays himself with the expensive French perfume, a glass urn of amber liquid marked Guerlain with the unmistakable whiff of vanilla.

He opens the windows and stands on the marble windowsill. He can see the lights of Florence in the valley below, the sheen of the Duomo. How could you get tired of this? he wonders. He has never felt so opulent, so himself. He smokes a cigarette, flicks the butt down onto the street.

He rubs cold cream onto his face and, letting it sit awhile, begins sifting through Romaine's drawers. In the top drawer of her bureau he finds yellowed photographs, and one which immediately stands out from the rest. It is not a beautiful photograph. Here, in some studio, some mansion from another time, another life, there is a boy in Victorian breeches seated on a tasseled velvet pillow. The boy has a wild dog's eyes and long, tangled blond hair. Mario shudders and places the photograph back in the drawer.

At 3:00 a.m., still wearing her pajamas, he

wheels Romaine to the toilet, then to the guest room and helps her to bed, turning back the heavy duvet, easing Romaine's diminished body underneath the sheets.

What are you wearing? she asks, wincing, her eyelids swollen. She reaches out to touch him with a finger. Why are we in the guest room?

He notices her nails are long and need trimming. Shh, he says. You're imagining things.

It's late, she says. My back hurts. Do you have pills? I need pills.

Shh, he says, turning off the lights and leaving her as quickly as possible. He sleeps in her bed and wakes slowly and contentedly in the linen sheets.

In the morning, Mario makes what he considers to be decent eggs and perfectly crisped bacon and takes the food to Romaine.

Why am I in the guest bedroom? she asks, narrowing her eyes.

We're having work done in your room, he says. You recall the damp spot on the ceiling?

Have you found a replacement chef? she asks, frowning at the tray, the yolks running across the china. Someone competent? These are vile eggs. I once knew a blind peasant who could cook better than this.

I'm looking. I want the best for you, Mario says. Then he says her name: Romaine.

Signora.

Yes. Signora.

You can take the tray downstairs. I don't want breakfast.

That afternoon she wraps her old fingers around his arm with surprising strength as they are sitting in the parlor. I want to end my life, she says plainly. Surely we can pay someone? A doctor who has a gambling debt? There must be a black market for these things? I can't be the only one tired of living?

I'll look into it, Mario says, though he has no intention of helping her end her life. If she were to die, he'd lose the beautiful house, the opera cape, the fine wine, the respite from his mother.

The next morning a nice woman with short hair and round cheeks named Berthe shows up at the house. Mario answers the door.

I'm just off the train from Paris, she says, smiling.

Signora does not take visitors, he says gravely.

I have news from a gallery, she says. Since

136

Romaine won't answer the letters, Natalie sent me in person.

Begrudgingly, Mario heads upstairs to inform Romaine of her visitor.

Tell her she is not to come unannounced, Romaine says, voice as loud as he's ever heard it. Tell her I don't read letters from Natalie's spies!

She says your work will be displayed at a prominent exhibition in Paris, Mario says.

Tell her I don't care. Tell her I'm dead.

When Mario tells Berthe that Romaine will not see her, Berthe looks down at her feet, then bites her lip, speechless.

Two hours later, when Mario takes out the trash, Berthe is still sitting on the old stone wall in front of the villa.

She thinks we're all out to hurt her, she says. Won't you tell her she can trust me? That I mean her no harm? All we want to do is secure the legacy she deserves.

Mario shrugs his shoulders. I'll tell her, he says.

I served her lunch nearly every day for twenty years, Berthe says, dumbfounded, on the brink of tears, hands gripping her knees.

Mario nods curtly at her. She is a threat, someone who might genuinely care for Romaine and threaten his job, his newfound freedom. When he peers out of Romaine's blinds before supper, Berthe is gone.

Another letter comes from Natalie, which he doesn't share with Romaine but reads alone, reclining on the couch downstairs: *My Angel is, as ever, first in my thoughts and deepest in my heart.*

It's hard for Mario to imagine Romaine deep in anyone's heart. He stares at the lavender card stock with disbelief and jealousy. He wants words this intense, this loving, coming in a letter with his name on it. But he's never been in love. Only once, perhaps, with a man who was twice his age, a teacher who kissed him behind the changing rooms at the swimming pool one summer, sticking his tongue in his mouth, amidst the blooming flowers and buzzing insects. Mario was fourteen and wrote the man at least fifteen letters and he responded only once, telling him to go to hell and leave him alone.

Mario falls asleep with Natalie's letter on his chest. When he wakes up he notices the dust floating through the house, settling on the expensive, unused furniture slipcovered in white muslin. He hasn't checked on Romaine in some time. Regretfully, he goes to her with a tray of tea and a stale croissant.

Please draw for me again, he tells her.

Absolutely not. You're late. I've been sitting here, waiting. I shouldn't have to wait in my own house.

If you want pills, you'll draw, Mario says calmly, leaning on the table, feeling as though he can afford to be casual.

I won't stand for this! she crows. I'll tell —

Who will you tell? Your mind is slipping. You're confused, darling. You want pills?

Mario has no idea what pills Romaine wants, or how to find a doctor on the black market, but he knows she wants both badly. He spreads his palm across Romaine's shoulder.

Do I have your word about the pills? she asks, her voice defeated.

You have my word, he says, handing her the pen.

He watches as the lines turn into a Pegasus-like figure, with the same bald demons she'd drawn earlier gripping its tail, holding on to the winged horse as if it were a balloon they could ride into the sky. Looking at the simplicity of her drawing, he tries his own hand at the figures.

Stop, Romaine says impatiently, looking over at his work. You have no talent.

But if I practice . . .

Romaine doesn't hesitate: Not even then. You have no sense of depth or feeling, there is nothing jarring in your line.

A line is a line, isn't it?

It is *not,* she says, laughing meanly at his ignorance. There is so much behind a line. You see simplicity where there is much more at work. People like you —

Would you teach me?

He can feel the new film of self-confidence he has acquired peeling back, revealing the well of self-doubt, the sense he has carried with him his entire life that he has been wronged, that he is owed more. He needs her to see who he really is, who he can become. He hates her and he needs her love, and she is never going to give it.

You aren't sufficiently traumatized, Romaine explains, one hand in the air. Teaching you would be a waste of time. I can look at you and tell. Accept it now and save yourself the trouble.

He leaves abruptly, taking the tray with him. He can hear her laughing. His ears sting.

One August morning there is vigorous knocking at the front door. He looks out the window and sees two well-dressed people, a man and a woman, waiting.

Romaine! the man yells. We're here!

Mario, caught off guard, locks the bedroom door and quickly changes out of the pink pajamas, panting nervously. He tries to straighten the dressing table and knocks over the perfume.

Where did they come from? Who called them? How does she have any friends left?

He rushes downstairs to open the door.

May I help you? he asks, aware that he reeks of vanilla.

We're here to move Romaine to Nice, the man says, brushing past him.

Soon there are cardboard boxes, crates for the paintings, radios blaring pop songs and news about factory strikes and student protests, men sweating on the staircase. The friends are in *his* house. They are causing confusion and disarray.

Gray and Michele are in their mid-sixties, elegant, artistic, grossly cheerful. At night they leave the house to go drinking. No one will say it, Mario thinks, but they must know it's the last move, the final time they'll be called upon.

Romaine is silent, brooding, staring out the window as people move around her, rolling up carpets. She is thinner than ever, not eating.

Once, as Gray is talking about his lackluster watercolors, Mario pipes up, hopeful to join the conversation. I'm a failed artist too, he says.

You never had any art to fail, Romaine says.

The quiet is so excruciating that Mario is forced to think of a task. He nods humbly and stumbles out to the patio, which he sweeps furiously, more thoroughly than ever before.

On her last day at Villa Gaia, Romaine requests a lunch of cold tongue followed by semolina pudding. Michele, glamorous in a pink sheath dress, offers her a glass of verdicchio.

Romaine waves her off. Pink clothes are vulgar, she says, shielding her eyes.

While Mario is preparing the lunch trays, a carabiniere marches up the front stairs in his crisp blue uniform and hat and knocks on the door. Mario answers.

The lady of the house called to report a theft, he says.

Mario covers his mouth with a hand. There's been no theft, he says.

I must be thorough, the carabiniere says. You understand.

Let me show you to her, Mario says, heart pounding. Signor, he says, before entering the room, you should know that her mental powers are greatly diminished. She's moving to Nice tomorrow, and gets very confused. But it's kind of you to humor her.

Mario stands in the doorway as the carabiniere greets Romaine.

The boy has been stealing from me, Romaine says, pointing a finger at Mario. He thinks I don't know what he's doing.

No, no, Officer, Mario hears himself saying. There was a cook here who had some debts. He was fired and left angrily, taking the wine and God knows what else.

Yes, Michele says, stepping forward. Our Romaine can be a little paranoid. She has visions.

The carabiniere smiles. It's a smile that says, *Yes, I'm in on this joke. Poor old rich woman with five locks on the door.*

But should the carabiniere choose to search the flat Mario shares with his mother, he would not find a stolen painting. He would not find anything unless he looks inside Mario's mother's Bible, where she has stashed Romaine's drawings because she thinks they are evil. *Lavoro del diavolo*, she said, plucking them from his wall. He brings them home, the few times he has deigned to spend a night outside of Romaine's elegant bedroom. He's kept all but the one he sold to the dealer, the money from which he will use to rent a room in

Saint-Tropez. He was tempted to sell more, but it felt like a transgression, even against Romaine, and he loved the feeling of possessing her work.

He can picture Saint-Tropez now: a lover in his bed, the glittering sea, the green hills, the masts of tall boats, the women in their wide-brimmed hats and enormous sunglasses. He will be standing in a window, watching them all.

The carabiniere bids them good afternoon. Hours later, Michele and Gray have gone out drinking, and Mario is home alone with Romaine. He takes his favorite cape from the closet, gently folds it, and places it into a paper bag.

Romaine is having her dinner, hands trembling as she runs her knife through the tongue, leftovers, which she has never deigned to eat before now. But tonight is different from other nights.

I do not care for her, Mario thinks. I do not feel sorry for her. I only want to take some small slice of her life and have it for myself.

He comes to the chair and crouches down at her knees, which he has done so many times.

Can I wash your hair?

Why must you be so tender about everything? she asks, dropping her utensils to the
plate. It's unnerving.

He moves silently about the room, adjusting the black curtains, waiting.

It would be nice to be clean before I
travel, she says flatly.

He fills the tub with warm, not hot, water.
He opens the small window in the bathroom
and lets the fresh air in. He helps Romaine
undress, steadying her as he unbuttons her
blouse, never making eye contact. When she
nearly slips he lifts her up like a young bride
and lowers her carefully into the soapy water.

The dog is barking. The motorbikes
scream underneath the window. This is what
his mother does, he thinks, washing something that belongs to someone else. Romaine
sits in the tub with her knees up. Relax, he
says. Let go.

I can't.

You must. You should.

He grips each side of her face with his
hands. It won't hurt, he says.

She is staring at him — or she may be
looking through him onto someone else,
someone he can't see — with those eyes.
One trails off, the other remains steadily on
his face, searching. The night comes.

Hazel Marion Eaton Watkins performing on Hager's Wall of Death, 1927. **Photo originally published in the**

Portland Sunday Telegram, *March 12, 1939.*

HAZEL EATON AND
THE WALL OF DEATH

1921

She survives by telling herself not to think.

Just do. Just move. Just balance. Forget yourself.

She often feels as if she leaves her body before a performance and returns to it when her motorcycle is still and her feet are planted on the ground.

But sometimes not thinking means death, or almost death, and today she's lying in a hospital room in Bangor, in and out of consciousness, with facial lacerations, broken ribs, a fractured femur, and a concussion, which happened when her rear brake locked up as she was circling the motordrome at sixty miles per hour. She slid down the wall like grain pouring from a sack, fast and haphazard, with her heavy bike following her body, pinning her leg.

Shit, she thinks. I'm going to throw up.

Now she knows the sound of an audience's

149

horror, and it is different than rapt joy and amazement. And so she's left alone for the moment, watching clouds move beyond the windowpane, and realizes that she's afraid. Fear, in the past, has been something she can turn off, but she can't find the energy today to move it aside.

It's only when she's afraid that she second-guesses her decisions, and it's only when she second-guesses her decisions that she thinks of her daughter, Beverly, who lives in Vermont with Hazel's mother.

Am I a terrible person for giving her up?

"I'm cold," she says, but her face is bandaged and she can only moan. She tries to rub her arms, but maybe one of them is broken, and then she's out again, riding a morphine high into nothingness.

Out of that nothingness emerges the candy-striped lighthouse at West Quoddy Head in Lubec, Maine, where she was born, the easternmost point in the United States, a beautiful, lonely, and snow-drenched place where her father dutifully tended the light to keep schooners from crashing into the jagged rocks, hidden by fog banks and dark nights.

She can still hear the boom of the fog cannon, still smell lard oil and kerosene on her father's hands. Many of their belongings —

mirrors, clocks, the silver tea set — took on a crusty salinity. She frequently cut her feet on the barnacled rocks, swam out into swirling currents because she was bored.

She had loved her parents but not the long stretches of loneliness; days in the keeper's cottage were too quiet, too monotonous, and she ran away at fifteen to join the Johnny Jones Exposition.

She thinks of those first weeks, the vigor of the itinerant carnival life, how seductive the sounds and smells were after years of looking out over the Bay of Fundy. There was gregarious music and conversation, the burnt sugar smell of cotton candy, and the savory smell of meat roasting. God, the only live music she heard the first years of her life was the calls of loons, the tinkling of sailboats, the whinnies of horses, the rhythm of waves. She'd craved volume, intensity, action, and Johnny had put her in a high-dive act, which, a few dives in, had also landed her in this very hospital, when she struck her head and split her scalp down to the bone. That's when she took to the motorcycle.

"Who recovers on a motorcycle?" her mother had asked, hysterical.

She never wore a helmet, even when she could feel the wind rushing over the bald spot on her head where the stitches were. You couldn't let fear in, she figured, and a helmet was one way of admitting the anticipation of being hurt, of breaking. A helmet acknowledged your vulnerability.

There is coughing nearby, the sound of another gurney's wheels squealing over the waxed wooden floor. Someone down the hall is going on and on about President Harding's poker habit.

"Stop," she mumbles, injuries throbbing. "I need quiet."

She retreats into her memories, and recalls the way a storm looked as it approached the lightkeeper's house, the way you had to brace yourself for the onslaught of waves and wind because the house was literally on the edge of the island; she could stare down into the opaque sea from her bedroom window, which the wind rattled and flew underneath, chilling her even on summer nights. Her father would tend the light no matter how bad the gales got. Even during hurricanes, he ran up and down the winding wrought-iron stairs. She remembers the sound of his feet, the clunk-clunking, the urgency. Through him she learned what stupid devotion to a task feels like, repetitive motion. She lives it. Around and around the motordrome she lives it, her slender foot on the gas.

A brisk, starched nurse stands over her for a minute and feels for her pulse. Her fingers are rough and warm.

"Don't tell my parents," Hazel slurs, but the nurse is gone. Her parents will see reports of the crash in the papers anyway, and her mother will write her a letter asking, *Why? Why must you put yourself in harm's way every week? Every day?*

What they don't know: nothing has topped the feeling of standing next to the motordrome, smiling into the din of applause. Nothing has topped the way men shake her hand and look her in the eye, what it's like to be able to call a man chickenshit to his face and get away with it, to mean it, to feel free and dominant and in control of your life.

I'll fight my way back to that vital feeling, she thinks. I will raise the stakes, put a lion in my sidecar like they do down in Alabama.

Her coastal life had been full of loons, gulls, rocks, and maps. "We're the first to see the sunrise at the equinox," her mother had reminded her, as if this alone was compelling enough to keep a family isolated from society, tending a light day in and day out.

The sunrise is beautiful, Hazel had

thought then, but it will never be enough. She was questioning then, as she does now: what makes you empty and what makes you full?

The morphine is a tidal wave of warmth through her body. She shudders. Her eyes are closed, but she can sense light, a sort of redness seeping in through her lids. She's living now in the interior of her mind, and there is the familiar view of looking up, forty-nine feet up, at the twisting staircase that leads to the blinding light. Tend it; do not look into it.

What do my daughter's eyes look like? she wonders, thinking back to the moment when the screaming child had slid from her body, the child that could have changed everything, if she'd let her, and she had not let her. The first time she held the child she'd let her fingers rest on the baby's soft spot, the place where the skull had not yet closed over the pulsing brain.

There's also the familiar view of looking up from the cylindrical wall of death, the sensation of seeing people but not knowing them as individuals, never catching their eyes.

The audience is looking down, she thinks, or is it my father? I am looking up. I am spinning. I am fast but not empty. I am swimming in the strong currents near the jetties, I am crying with the gulls, bobbing like the buoy on a lobster trap, looking through the fog banks over the churning Bay of Fundy.

Allegra Byron, illegitimate daughter of Lord Byron and Claire Clairmont, 1817.

THE AUTOBIOGRAPHY OF ALLEGRA BYRON

On the first of March, 1821, Allegra Byron entered the Convento di San Giovanni like a small storm, accompanied by nonrelations, overdressed women who handled her with cool affection. It was a clear morning, so we met our charge in the prayer garden, a patch of grass where a few ancient olive trees were waking up to spring. Though lauded by her guardians as an early talker, three-year-old Allegra greeted us with silence.

This, her chaperone said, is your new home.

Allegra looked at our faces, then the grounds and buildings. I don't like it, she said.

I stood with another Capuchin sister, flanking the abbess, who lorded over the garden with a solemn stare. A breeze whipped our brown habits around our knees, exposing our humble shoes. I felt my job was to soften the harsh presence of the abbess. These moments, when a child was left in our care, struck me as pivotal in the child's life.

The convent was not a place of peace; it was a place of noise, an almost holy sanctuary carved out in the heart of Bagnacavallo in northeast Italy. It was a boarding school, repository for unwanted children, and abbey for Capuchin nuns. The surrounding buildings were a pastiche of gray-, cream-, and flesh-colored bricks and plaster; the streets were irregular and winding and smelled of thick peasant soups. Soon the convent gardens would be tilled and planted with lettuces and herbs that could withstand late frosts.

Vendors set up leather, vegetable, and paper carts underneath our public arches. The Roma curled their dirty fingers around our iron gates — *a little something, gaje,* they said to anyone looking — but we were not allowed to help them. I could smell garlic, pungent and a little sweet, burning in the trattorias on my afternoon walks past the Palazzo Gradenigo to the boundary of Porta Pieve, the town gate. At night, from my cold bed, I could hear the syncopated rhythm of horse hooves on via Garibaldi's cobblestone when all else was still.

I'd come to Bagnacavallo the year before Allegra arrived, the month my newborn daughter and husband died from typhus. My milk was still strong, and I wanted to be put to use. I wanted to be occupied, exhausted, sucked dry. I wanted to cut myself off from everything outside of the convent walls.

Say hello, Allegra, her chaperone urged.

The girl's eyes were large chestnut jewels, insouciant below ash-blond curls. Her chin was dimpled, giving her face a strange maturity. Her empire-waist muslin dress, which peeked out beneath her unbuttoned velvet coat, was wrinkled from constant movement. Instead of pleasantries, the girl marched off to shake an olive tree, leaving footprints in what remained of a late snow.

Allegra is prone to fevers and tantrums, the lead chaperone said. She likes to drink warm milk and eat biscuits in the evenings. Her father requests that —

We have biscuits, the abbess said, turning to project her voice toward the girl. The abbess was a formidable woman of sixty-eight with short gray hair she cut herself. She was tall, humorless, and deeply committed to the church.

Amaretti? Allegra asked, the question shaping the bow of her cupid's mouth.

The abbess nodded, but I'd never encountered amaretti in the convent. It was my first notion that the girl was being won over in front of her charges, that she was a prize. This was not the type of place that made cookies or catered to whims. The sisters were thin. Righteous, they ate like sick birds.

I could tell immediately that Allegra was a difficult child, but something in me felt I could reach her. I watched her quietly, the way she pretended to play while eyeing her chaperones' every move. Her anxiety was evident. She moved to clutch at the knees of the lead chaperone.

At the convent I'd nearly found what I was searching for: blankness. I sought exhaustion through labor, a mind quieted by industriousness.

When I arrived in Bagnacavallo, they'd given me the problem children — the ones yellow with malaria or wild with seizures. My first six months, I nursed a countess's discarded son to health, despite his severe cleft palate, which wrenched his lip into his nostril like a drawn curtain. I stroked his thick black hair and rubbed his cheek with my callused thumb, watched his chest rise, his stomach swollen with milk.

Early on, one of the Capuchin sisters gave

me a warning. Your first instinct at the orphanage is to possess a child, she said, to make it love you best.

But guard your heart, *mia cara,* she said, her habit the color of light coffee, faded from coarse hand washing. When the children you've suckled are grown, they will forget you. When the children you've taught go home, they will hate you as if you're the one who kept them here.

In the nursery, you could get away with the luxury of affection. But as soon as the children became toddlers, the tone sterilized, as if reticence and decorum were more instructional than compassion.

The nursery walls were a sickly green, and there was, I worried, malice in our Madonna's face. She stood with her hands out and open on a wooden table. Her fingers were too thin; her hair, too gold; her lips, too red.

Hail Mary, full of grace, I said that evening before dinner, rosary in hand at the Madonna's feet. *Blessed is the fruit of thy womb . . .*

You could tell she hadn't enough mercy for all of us. Perhaps it had been siphoned off years ago. Perhaps there wasn't much to begin with.

I did not see Allegra again until bath time, when I left the sleeping infants in the nursery to assist with turndown rituals for the older children. As my milk had dried the month before, I'd been asked to make the transition from the nursery to the boarding facilities.

I manned my station, a tin tub on a wooden floor, the bathwater a little dirty but warm. Allegra was undressed and handed to me. The rims of her eyes were red with fatigue. I set her down next to the bath. She looked at the water, then pressed her feet — still plump with baby fat — against the tub and shot backward, the skin of her bottom taut against the cold floor.

No! she screamed, smacking her naked heels on the wooden floors. *Lo non voglio un bagno!* Her words echoed off the walls and tall ceiling as if she were calling from the top of the Alps, unholy and alarming sounds.

Allegra fell into a wild tantrum, her nostrils flared, her back arched. Her little body was a wonder, stout and athletic. She threw herself across the floor, kicking the air. No, she screamed. No.

Shh, *mia cara,* I whispered. Shh, Shh.

I brought her to her feet, placed one arm around her chest, kneeled behind her, and tried to contain her. Her arms flailed and one struck me in the nose, sending tears to my eyes. I was afraid she would hurt herself. Her body went slack. The other children watched, wide-eyed.

Ten minutes more and I will call for an exorcism, the sister beside me said.

It's her first night, I said.

Mammina, Mammina, Allegra wailed. Her breathing was jagged. Papa.

She now stood a few feet from the tub, her eyes shut and mouth gasping for air between sobs. She urinated on the floor, watery beads sliding down her solid legs. No, she screamed. No bath!

Shh, shh, I said. If you will bathe like a good girl, I said, taking her hand, we will make a letter for Papa.

She continued to cry but let me move her into the tub. She sat still, like a stone cherub in a fountain, her face a tableau of misery. Her blond curls flattened to her shoulders and neck as I poured a cup of dull water over her head.

I washed her quickly and not without tenderness. I lifted one arm, then the other, enamored with their girth and proportion. As I raised her from the tub and began to towel-dry her hair, she started to wail again. Her cry was sharp and unpleasant, like that of a bleating sheep lost from the herd, and everything in me wanted it to stop.

Take me home, she begged, casting herself forward over my arm. Take me home.

Hush, I said. You must calm down.

Her eyes looked past me. I picked her up off the floor. She kicked and clawed at me and slid down my frame as I repeatedly bent to find a better hold. Darkness was coming in through the windows, and we were losing precious visibility. The convent was too large to light in entirety.

Allegra's young skin was like marzipan, her cheeks scrubbed and shiny like the *frutta martorana* the cafés served at Christmas. I wrapped her tightly in a towel, whisked her down the hallway to the bedchamber.

The bedroom for three- and four-year-old girls — there were six of them — was small, but the ceiling rose to enormous heights, capped off in a Gothic arch, humbling everything beneath it with space and shadow. As soon as Allegra's body went limp with exhaustion, I pulled a nightgown over her head. Her eyes opened once, blank. I ran a comb through her hair and tucked her underneath the sheets, which smelled of lye. The beds were donated from a hospital, undersized wrought-iron frames that sat upon the old floor unevenly.

Try to sleep, I whispered, touching her small back, feeling its heat. I'll see you in the morning.

I had a chill as I made my way back to clean the bath station; the fight with Allegra had dampened my clothes and hair. I crouched to mop the spilled water around the tub. The horsehair packed between the cracks of the wood flooring occasionally came loose, dirtying my rag.

The abbess approached me. I saw her worn shoes first, then looked up to meet her eyes. Sister, she said. You broke protocol this evening putting Allegra to bed.

She was upset, I said. I thought —

There are no favorites here, she said. Consider this a warning.

It had always been my intention at the convent to be nobody, to go unnoticed, to punish myself until I could no longer feel the weight of my dead child in my arms. But the old fight in me stirred, the fight of a peasant's wife who had sewn seeds in the hills of Alfonsine while pregnant, tended my ill husband a day after childbirth. I swallowed the protest and continued drying the floor.

Mother of Mercy, our life, our sweetness, and our hope, I mumbled. *To thee do we cry, poor banished children of Eve; to thee do we send up our sighs . . .*

Prayers were dead songs lodged in my

head, soothing, routine words that meant less to me than they should have.

That night my room — one that looked like all the others, with whitewashed walls, a cracked plaster ceiling, and a small bed — smelled damp. I went to bed with a body of glass, tired and aching for the child I'd lost. At least it was she who had abandoned me.

Across the convent, we knew what we weren't supposed to know, that Allegra was the illegitimate daughter of the notorious poet George Gordon, Lord Byron, and his mistress, Claire Clairmont. A sister had overheard Allegra's chaperones gossiping with the abbess in her lamplit chambers. The abbess was merely a receptacle for such talk, never engaging in it herself.

He *does* believe her to be his child, one said. The likeness is there, as is the temper, and it's the temper he can no longer stand. Perhaps from that estranged, godless mother —

She's only *three,* the other chaperone said, exasperated. One can only expect so much from a child who's lived all over the country with four families in so many years.

The chaperone had tears in her eyes. We don't want to see her go, she said. She so loves her papa.

The child will be fine, the abbess assured her. She'll receive an excellent education, both spiritual and academic.

But will she be loved? one chaperone asked the other as they turned to leave.

Either the abbess did not hear her or she did not wish to speculate.

I saw Allegra a few evenings later at mealtime. I looked forward to dinner every night — the soft, solemn chatter and bowed heads, the clanking of silverware. Allegra had not touched the spaghetti on her plate, and as I walked past she raised her hand to get the attention of the sister who was manning her table.

More milk, she said. And then, with a voice that was at once sugared and wicked, added: *please.*

Allegra's manners were affected and her face did not show residual infancy like those of her peers. Now that we knew who she was, we attributed intelligence to her eyes and remarks. Early on she wielded intimidating power over the sisters. No one wanted to instigate one of her notorious tantrums or become the object of her dislike.

I was drawn to her face, the life within it, the light underneath her skin.

The letter, Sister, she said, in a childish but articulate voice, catching my sleeve. I want to write a letter to Papa. You promised. During the bath.

The sisters had already received instructions that no one but the abbess was allowed to contact Lord Byron directly.

We'll begin tomorrow, I said. I'll find you before prayers.

I did not know if I would be permitted to send her letters, but I knew we would write them. An academic exercise, I told myself.

As I turned to leave Allegra's side, I heard one of the older boys at a neighboring table speculate on the existence of the Capuchin Crypt. The boys' eyes still sparkled; they ran down the halls when no one was looking. They did not break as quickly as the girls.

And underneath the churches in Rome, he said, there are thousands of skulls and rotting bodies of friars. Their bones are nailed to the walls, and they make chandeliers from the skulls, candles in the eye sockets.

Allegra's eyes were wide. She was leaning forward, taking in the boy's words, though how much she understood was hard to guess. At three, nearly four, she inhabited the space between a baby and a child, far more interested in the older kids than in the benign beings at her own table.

Is that what happens to our bodies if we die here? the boy asked the sister at his table. Our bones are nailed to the walls? Candles are lit inside our heads?

No one is dying here, the sister said, though we all knew it wasn't true. People were dying everywhere.

Even inside the convent walls we felt the threat of typhus and malaria, the stress and strain of political turmoil. We washed our hands raw. The last of winter was still upon us and we did not have full gardens or a lemon harvest to take our thoughts away from the unrest. Though the Carbonari insurrections and violence were worse in the south, there were revolutionaries in our hills — the Adelfia and Filadelfia. Just last month the Austrians had crossed the Po, upsetting Italy's unification advocates. One had the feeling that Italy did not yet know itself, and more blood would be shed in its quest to become whole.

Do not let strangers in, the abbess instructed, and do not leave the grounds unless absolutely necessary. The Carbonari are anticlerical, and we do not know what or whom they would use to make a point.

That afternoon, after Allegra had received her lessons, we sat together in the cafeteria, light streaming through tall, thin windows. A dinner of *ribollita* and *piselli* was being prepared. The cooks, I knew, were dumping the week's leftovers into a pot with tomatoes and bread to make a thick soup. I could smell the onions frying on the cast iron.

Tell me, I said, what you want to say to your papa.

Dear Papa, she began, her lovely face racked with concentration. There are no amaretti and I do not receive evening milk here. I want to come home now.

Allegra could not yet read. She looked at the paper — a used sheet of music I'd found with one blank side — eagerly.

She watched my hand as I wrote: *Dear Papa, I am happy here but miss you dearly. Please bring amaretti when you come.*

Knowing the abbess would not be pleased with the letter's contents, I edited the text.

Allegra's blond hair was pinned into a simple knot. She was thinner, I felt, than when she had come; she had not eaten much since arriving. Her knees bounced.

Now, she said, pointing to the page, tell him that I like singing. If he visits, I will sing for him. I will sing "God the Son" and "*O Salutaris Hostia.*"

I did as instructed and ended the letter: *Con affetto, Allegra.*

Now, I said, patting her small hand. Off to prayers. She trailed behind me as we walked to the chapel, the convent's bells tolling the hour of four, reverberating in our chests. As we reached the great doors, Allegra touched the back of my leg, pausing for a moment, gathering herself before she joined the other children.

I wanted to cup her small head in my hands, crouch low, kiss her worried forehead. I wanted to bring her to my hip, tell her a funny story, play with her hair. But I did not touch her, and let the girl go running down the center aisle alone, blond hair bouncing, the travertine loud underneath the soles of her feet.

In August, just as the walls of the convent began to pulse with the sun's heat, Allegra received a visit from the poet Percy Bysshe Shelley, a thin man with feminine cheekbones and burning eyes.

He was immediately affectionate with her, hugging her and kissing her forehead, though her stiffness indicated that she did not remember him. He'd come to us while we were seated in the cafeteria for our morning chat, escorted by the abbess, who receded into the background.

She's pale, he whispered to me, nodding at Allegra. What is she fed?

What everyone else is fed, I answered. Soups, bread, meat, vegetables.

Allegra was inserting spoons into stacks of cloth napkins, in a manner that was industrious and childlike at the same time.

Why doesn't she speak more? he asked.

She speaks plenty, I said, trying to reassure him. She's one of our most precocious students.

Tell your friend, the abbess boomed from the shadows at Allegra, what you learn here.

Jesus, Allegra said, prayed in the Garden of Gethsemane. His sweat became blood.

Can you recite the Apostles' Creed for your friend? the abbess said, a note of pride in her voice, as if she was eager for Shelley to report Allegra's progress to her father.

I believe in God, the Father almighty. Allegra looked up at Shelley's eyes, perhaps sensing his horror. Her voice fell flat.

That won't be necessary, Shelley said, holding up one hand in protest. I'm quite confident in Allegra's capacity for recitation.

Shelley struck me as a nervous man, constantly running his fingers through his hair, a stream of energy and inquiry enlivening his body. I could sense his discomfort and wondered if he'd pictured another life for the girl, something more worldly and secular, a life hard for me to imagine.

Come, Allegra, he said, arms out. I've known you since you were a baby. We rolled billiard balls together once at your father's house. Do you remember?

Allegra remained coolly out of reach.

Do you see Mammina and Papa? she asked. Why have they not come for me?

The abbess took Allegra by the arm in her strong and sensible manner. It's time for prayers, she said, pulling the girl to her side. Say good-bye to your friend. Allegra moved compliantly, though she turned to stare at Shelley and me with wide brown eyes as she was led away.

Pardon the intrusive question, I said. But if you see her father, might you ask if he's open to receiving letters from his daughter? We have a rule against sending correspondence, but Allegra has written letters —

The poet nodded and was quiet for a minute, absorbing the visit.

She appears greatly tamed, Shelley said to me as the abbess and Allegra disappeared down the hall, though not for the better.

When her fourth birthday came, I checked

frequently, but nothing arrived for Allegra
— no gift, no letter, no word of a visit from
her father, his wife, or the girl's birth
mother.

We'd become as attached as the situation
would allow. When Allegra threw tantrums,
I was summoned. I was the only one who
could bathe her without incident. At first I
was cautious of showing favoritism, but I
began to see myself as a valued peacekeeper,
a problem solver. I convinced myself that
the abbess appreciated my efforts.

Did Allegra know it was her birthday? I
imagined she couldn't. The convent was a
timeless space; the institution achieved
comfort and righteousness in routine and
uniformity.

But I found Allegra crying outside of her
classroom, a sister standing over her. What's
wrong? I asked, aware of my own distress at
the girl's unhappiness.

The class wished Allegra a happy birthday
this morning, the sister said, a picture of
impatience in her brown habit.

And I could see, then, all the useless hopes
Allegra had been holding on to, the expecta-
tions she had. Her eyes were pink and tears
were smeared across her smooth cheeks.
Her hair, which had been pulled back from
her face, was mussed. She turned away from

me as I approached.

You're four today, I said, crouching beside her. I took her hand. Allegra buried her face between my bent knees.

I can manage Allegra for the morning, I told the sister. She looked relieved. Thank you, she said, disappearing quickly behind a wooden door, the whispers of her class ceasing quickly upon her reentry.

Last year, Allegra said, Papa brought a cake and a dress to my nursery.

And then I did the thing that I most regret and cherish. I opted not to soap the tubs, as was my weekly duty — they were cleaned each night after use and no one would notice — and instead indulged myself. I thought: What would please Him more — a clean tub, or this girl's happiness?

Would you like to go outside? I asked, touching Allegra's shoulder. Do something special?

Though it was forbidden to take children beyond the abbey walls, if I could get her to her seat in the cafeteria for lunch, I thought, there would be no suspicion, no problem.

Allegra's eyes lifted to mine and a smile began to form on her beautiful lips. She wiped her nose with the back of her hand. We moved quickly through the winding halls — the other children were in class or morning prayers — and to the kitchen, full of scalded pans, split tomatoes, and baskets of onions. The back door was the only unlocked door to the outside world. We walked through it. The cold air was fresh and rewarding. When I looked back at the abbey, the place seemed hollow, the windows black, as if there was nothing inside.

It wasn't unusual for a sister to be outside of the convent, but I knew the brown habit was still conspicuous, as was the skipping, beaming four-year-old in uniform beside me. Allegra became more alive in the winter sun. She held my hand tightly, jerking my arm as she occasionally lost her balance on the cobblestones. We caught glimpses of the blue sky above the buildings, which seemed taller and more jumbled than ever. Allegra kicked stray rocks and stared inside the *farmacias,* packed with colored jars and jugs and women out for morning errands.

Why is that man selling ugly hats? Allegra said. Why does that woman carry her groceries all alone? Does she not have children? How long did it take the men to build these streets?

So many questions without good answers, I said. Tell me what you think.

A hundred years to build the streets, she said.

I ran my fingers over the back of Allegra's hand. Her skin felt like a tulip petal, soft and undamaged. A vendor leaned forward with a bowl full of olives, tempting me to buy. Before I could pull her away, Allegra had one hand in the bowl, her fingers wrapped around three fat olives.

Allegra! I said.

Go ahead, the vendor said, laughing. Take them. *Nessun problema.*

She looked to me for permission, then brought the fruit to her mouth quickly, as if worried he would change his mind.

Allora, I said, kneeling on the cobblestone to take in the iridescent excitement in her eyes. Let's head to a café for an amaretti.

Her affection — even if it was fleeting and inconsistent — was a balm. Though I was nervous about breaking rules, the warmth that began to spread through my body was beautiful. The temporary freedom was intoxicating. I thought, then, about a place I could take Allegra. I thought about my childless aunt in her austere villa in Alfonsine, the extra bedrooms and lemon trees Allegra could climb.

But I knew I could not get away with such a scheme. I knew that while her father did not love her — not the way I could — he cared for her future. He wanted a formal education for Allegra, not a life sowing seeds alongside a peasant woman, a failed Capuchin sister. He wanted a dignified history and explanation, even for his illegitimate daughter.

I imagined making a case to him, a case based on my ability to love Allegra every day. I will ply her with wisdom and all the books I can get my hands on, I would say. We will memorize your texts . . .

I realized I had been making the case in my mind for weeks, imagining a life outside of the convent with Allegra as my own.

We reached a small piazza and entered Giuseppe's, a mirrored café that smelled of caramelized sugar and coffee. Paninis heaped with prosciutto and mozzarella were being stacked onto trays in preparation for lunch. Giuseppe's was a place for laborers and mothers, quiet and many turns off the main street. I brought Allegra to the counter.

A glass of warm milk for the little one, I said to the *cameriere,* and your best amaretti.

It's my birthday, Allegra said, unabashed. I'm four.

She did not savor the cookie but attacked it with childish vigor, plunging it into the milk.

I want to write a letter to Papa, she said to me, crumbs across her lip.

I don't have paper, I said, wiping her mouth with a cloth napkin.

Cameriere, Allegra called. Do you have paper?

He turned from fixing a cappuccino to stare at her.

I have a pamphlet, *mia cara,* he said. One I no longer want. *Politica stupida . . .*

And a pen? she said.

For you, he said, reaching behind the sacks of coffee to retrieve one. He handed it to me.

Your scribe, I presume, he said, nodding in my direction.

Dear Papa, Allegra began. Today I am four. Your gift did not arrive. I am learning my alphabet but do not like the food here.

She paused to press her finger into a crumb on the counter and pop it into her mouth. She continued: A boy says my right leg is longer than my left; I do not think this is true. Please come soon to bring me home.

Dear Papa, I wrote across the political pamphlet, ignoring the text beneath my ink. *I look forward to your next visit. I am learning my alphabet and wish to show you. Please come soon. Con affetto, Allegra.*

I reached into my habit to find the small sack of lire I kept hidden on my body at all times — we were not allowed to have money in the convent — and fished out coins to pay for Allegra's milk and cookie. We were running out of time.

I plucked her from her seat at the counter and held her for a moment. She wriggled down and burst out of the café. There was a fountain in the piazza, and she ran toward it.

In the middle of the fountain was a stone horse bucking into the air, his front legs raised in high alert. Water dribbled from the horse's mouth. It sounded like a small stream as it hit the tea-colored pool beneath.

Allegra! I shouted. We do not have time! *Arrestare!*

She did not turn back.

Two men on horseback came between us. For a moment I could hear the abbess's cautionary words, and I became fearful that Allegra would be hurt or taken from me. I was upset at myself for not being more careful, for putting the girl's life in jeopardy.

Allegra! I said. Stay where you are.

She was faster than I. As I hurried toward her she looked back once and smiled at me, and if it was a wicked smile, or the smile of a happy child who had forgotten herself,

I'm not sure — but she placed one leg into the fountain.

Do not —

She swung her other leg over the stucco ledge and stood knee-deep in the cold, dirty water. She began to splash. She scooped water with her hands and thrust it into the air and over her blond head. She laughed.

I reached the fountain and pulled her backward over the ledge, planting her two feet on the gray cobblestone. Her clothing dripped and sagged, and she began to cry.

Knowing now that we would be caught, I slung her over my shoulder and began to walk. She kicked and beat my shoulder, but I was resolute and strong and walked further than I believed I could with her body draped over me.

I was reminded, then, of my mother's assertion that you must work for love. Allegra's love, I knew, was not mine to have. There was no obligation, no blood, no history that made it so. But even then, as something inside of me raged at her impulsiveness, a thing like love stirred. I didn't want to turn her over to the abbey again. I wanted to brush her hair, put her in a warm bed, tell her a story about the shepherd in Bergamo who lost his sheep, the one my mother used to tell me, her eyes big and her voice hushed.

The last block my back began to ache and I could no longer carry Allegra. Her body was cold, and I knew the walk would be good for her circulation. She had calmed and, once placed on the cobblestone, held my hand obediently, as if aware we were facing trouble.

It was quiet in the city. A few articles of laundry waved from the balconies above us. The sand-colored facades seemed to close in around us as we walked. For the first time, I realized the columns that held the upper stories of the buildings above us were painted the color of dried blood.

The only way into the convent was through the kitchen door. The cooks stopped their chatter and chopping as we entered, the air around them pungent and much warmer than the temperature outside. Allegra's wet hair curled over her shoulders, and she began to shiver.

I kept her hand in mine and we walked to the dormitory. I did not make eye contact with anyone; I was focused on getting Allegra into dry clothes.

Later that evening, after the rumors had spread, one of the sisters came to my room. "The abbess will see you now," she said.

■ ■ ■ ■

When Allegra's first fever came on, I was unable to go to her, though I was told she asked for me. The abbess, infuriated at my poor decision, had not expelled me.

You'll serve the Reparto Speciale indefinitely, she said. Under close supervision.

The Reparto Speciale was a dark wing of the convent, the place where only truly disturbed girls were kept, some chained to their beds, some refusing food, some maimed from experimental surgeries and unable to feed themselves. I fed them broth, their eyes gurgling with a wildness I could not fathom. I changed their sheets and clothes. Some spoke in tongues; some did not speak at all. I was bitten, besieged by prying fingers, hit in the chest with a bedpan. Once a week I filed their nails, which many of them bit down to jagged quicks or, in fits of rage, used to scratch the corneas of their caretakers in protest of a linen change. There were four patients per room, and I read scripture to them before turning down their gas lamps.

I did not dare stop by the infirmary on the way to my room at night; I'd been given strict instructions to avoid Allegra. Still, I imagined her shaking and sweating underneath rough blankets, delirious, lonely. Her father did not come to her bedside; through letters, I was told, he claimed to feel certain of her strong constitution and recovery.

When I lay in bed at night, I could still picture the eyes of my newborn daughter, freshly and forever closed, her eyelashes long and lush, her skin yellowed, her life abbreviated. Her eyes, at death, were certainly more peaceful than those of the girls I cared for, their breastbones protruding from thin gowns, their gnarled hands reaching toward the invisible.

Turn then, most gracious advocate, thine eyes of mercy toward us, and after this our exile, show unto us the blessed fruit of thy womb, Jesus. O clement, O loving, O sweet Virgin Mary . . .

I longed to be at Allegra's bedside. I knew that I could offer her comfort. But I would not risk further punishment, so I worked patiently, and waited.

Perhaps the abbess felt that I had served my time. Or perhaps Allegra had worn them down with her constant pleas. One month and thirteen days into my service in the Reparto Speciale, I was whisked to Allegra's bedside, where I found a cheerful four-year-old thumbing through a book.

I smiled, took her hand, and kissed her forehead. Tell me how you're feeling, *mia cara,* I said.

Can we go for another milk and *amaretti*? she asked.

And risk another swim in the fountain? I said. I think not.

Allegra smiled. Will you scratch my back? she asked, pointing to a place between her shoulders.

I knew that she would never love me, but I could delight, at least, in trust and familiarity.

We were allowed, then, to continue our daily visits before lunch. The abbess, I suppose, wanted to keep her sick, mercurial charge happy. Allegra and I always sat at the same table in the empty cafeteria. We continued to write letters to her father. They grew in length and content, and, with some exceptions, I tried to remain true to the author's intent.

Dear Papa, she instructed. *I now enjoy the spaghetti here. I have learned a great deal of Paradise and the angel Raphael. I would like very much for Mammina to bring me a toy and gold dress, and for you to visit and give me a hug and a kiss. How is your bad foot? I think I would like to have a bad foot too. Please visit your Allegra soon.*

I kept her letters by my bedside. The abbess would not give me permission to post them — I asked monthly — though I could, she said, present them to Byron at his next visit. There were now close to fifty letters, detailing Allegra's wishes for toys, her changing dietary preferences, remedial spiritual insights, and desire for visits from her family.

As we continued to compose the letters, week after week, my hardest job was convincing Allegra her father would read them.

Why does Papa not write back? she asked.

The mail is unreliable, I told her. Your father is a busy man who travels widely. But I know he loves you, and thinks of you fondly.

In February, the abbess received word that Byron might visit. There is some risk, she said, that the birth mother is living in the area and planning to kidnap Allegra from the convent. You'll keep a close watch, please.

I realized that if someone were to take Allegra from the convent and offer her a better life, I would not be entirely happy. I felt agitated by the news, and guilty at my own agitation. I did not want to give her up.

If Byron's visit is not certain, I told the abbess, I beg you not to get Allegra's hopes up.

She looked sternly at me, and I could tell my advice was not welcome. Her face was something I could not understand. It was weathered, tired. The compassion in her eyes, if that's what it was, was faded and rooted in an ancient system.

It would be good for him to visit, she said. Good for the convent.

And certainly good for Allegra, I said. But —

Perhaps we could post one of Allegra's letters to him, the abbess said. As encouragement.

I'll bring one to you in the morning, I said, excusing myself.

He wants to win a little favor, does he? one of the sisters asked me, as I left the abbess's dark quarters.

There are many things he could have done for her favor in the last year, I said. Out of simple decency, if not love.

The sister looked shocked. Excuse me, I said, eager to move on from the topic. I should not have spoken so openly.

In my room that night, I leafed through the stack of letters I had penned for Allegra. She'd begun to sign her name and contribute her own words, her handwriting large and unsteady. She had a tendency to bear down too hard on the paper, leaving little tears that she worried over.

Will Papa mind? she'd ask. Should we begin again?

I imagined Byron reading the letters of his progeny, halfheartedly entertained. Perhaps the matters on a genius's mind are bigger than little girls and their wants, bigger than dresses and circuses and cookies, early spiritual reckonings.

Not satisfied with the letters I had, I found Allegra in the morning as she was entering her classroom. Would you like to post a new letter to your papa? I asked.

Knowing this letter would reach him directly, I was determined to let her speak her mind. I promised myself that I would write down every word. Her teacher, one of the younger sisters, remained in the hallway, eager to help.

My dear Papa, Allegra said, stopping to hold her forehead.

I can't think, she said. My head hurts. What else should I say?

How about this? her teacher said. *It being fair time, I should like so much a visit from my papa as I have many wishes to satisfy. Won't you come to please your Allegrina, who loves you so?*

In your own words, Allegra, I said. Your own words are best.

I like the way she said it, Allegra said, nodding to the sister, who, impressed with her own eloquence, moved into the classroom, beckoning Allegra to join her, and she did.

Allegra's second fever hit fast. She began complaining of headaches and pain in her knees. She was sent to bed and assigned a full-time nurse. A doctor was summoned.

In the weeks prior, the convent had given shelter to a group of twelve men sent to us by Austrian authorities, soldiers perhaps, revolutionaries even, who had been found in a leaking boat off the coast of Grado. They were deloused and provided food, water, and beds. The doctor brought in to tend Allegra and others who had begun to show signs of rashes and fevers worried of a typhus outbreak. The abbess, however, insisted that Allegra's illness was related to her ongoing malarial fevers. Still, she wrote to Byron, who had not come to visit his daughter the entire length of her stay in Bagnacavallo.

Now he will come, she assured me.

Those days, between my visits to Allegra's

bed, prayer, and duties, I began to realize that I was more devoted to work than to Christ. I did, however, subscribe to the belief that I might find my own redemption through suffering, and looking at her sick body, I suffered. Listening to her groans of discomfort, I suffered. Feeling the weak grip of her fingers around mine, I suffered.

When will Papa come? she asked me.

He knows you are strong enough to wait, I said.

Byron did not come, nor did he write to us.

I spent long hours by Allegra's bedside, forgoing sleep as well as my duties. Her eyes rarely opened except when she asked for water. Her voice was small, and occasionally her arms flung themselves in unexpected directions during fitful sleep. I stroked her cheeks and told her stories from my childhood, the story of the shepherd from Bergamo.

Mammina, she said, her small lips devoid of all insolence and fight, just lips for drinking, lips for whispering small requests. Water. Papa.

Concerned that she did not show any signs of improving, the doctor ordered her bled. A vein in her right forearm was cut and ten ounces of blood were taken, then another fifteen in the evening. The process distressed me — it seemed to do nothing but weaken the child — so I left Allegra's bedside for the hour.

I set off for the café we had gone to together on her birthday. The same waiter was there, and I ordered an amaretti, removing the secret stash of lire from underneath my habit. I held the cookie gingerly, afraid it would crumble, so eager to present it to Allegra intact, though I knew she might not eat it.

Across the piazza, the fountain looked lonely, sustaining itself with a steady stream of water, filling and refilling, the stone horse and his rider made whole by the company of birds.

I could not help but remember my last encounter with death. When my own family died, I was alone with them for two days. Then my husband's brother arrived to help me bury the bodies, which I had laid out across the table, touching and crying over them until I could not bear to enter the room. We went to the backyard together and began to make holes in the rocky soil.

Two hours later I broke my shovel on the rocks and started digging with my hands. I wanted, then, to make room for myself. I dug until my fingers bled, until they pulled me out of the hole and begged me to sleep, the moon cold in the sky above us.

As I sat looking at Allegra, the tips of my fingers began to ache, and I knew it would not be long.

For three days Allegra was in pain, twisting and retching, sweating, clutching at her sheets, her eyes crushed shut, her hands damp.

Give her space, I told the nurses. And quiet.

A vigil had formed in the infirmary, composed of eight sisters, three doctors, and the abbess. They prayed until I no longer heard words, just the rhythm of words. I did not see their faces, just the movement of their brown habits in my peripheral vision.

After the gas lamps were turned down, most went to their rooms, but I stayed. I felt a strange burst of energy, the same energy I had felt in the days before my husband and daughter died, the compulsion to stay awake and soak in the last hours with those you love, to memorize the shapes of their bodies, the colors of their hair, their impression in the world.

Allegra, I said, touching her chest. Can

you hear me?

She did not respond, but took a breath and settled further into her bed. When Allegra fell into a deep rest — one where she breathed slowly and seemed only to inhabit a portion of her body — I was relieved that her suffering had ended, but I knew mine would begin again in earnest.

It was the twentieth of April and not quite warm when she gave up. She was pronounced dead at 10:00 p.m. The last amaretti remained at her bedside, untouched.

You should rest, the nurse told me, as they began to prepare Allegra's body, washing it, filing her small nails.

I shook my head, wanting to prolong the moment. I understood the finality of the situation and wanted to dwell, soak up the last of Allegra's spirit. I could see a crushing wave of sadness in front of me.

The abbess came to remove me, but, defiant with grief, I turned away. For hours I sat on a small chair next to Allegra until they took her. I touched her hair and imagined the trajectory of her life, willing her past the obstacle of death.

Lord Byron made a show of his grief and sent for her body as if it were a rare volume, the thing that had been missing from his library all along.

■ ■ ■ ■

A month later I moved to Murano, a small island outside of Venice, and became a washwoman for a glassmaker. I could not remain at Bagnacavallo; I was too angry, too tired, cynical.

You're making a mistake, the abbess said, when I told her my intentions.

I have made many, I said.

I lived away from the palazzos, where the gardens were beginning to bloom, and the scent of sea salt and pine filled the air.

I worked harder than I had worked before, trying to forget the children that had been taken from me. I requested extra shifts, thankful for the sleep that came after I'd exhausted myself.

During lunch I could not sit still. I ate baguettes and drank strong coffee. In the afternoons I made a habit of looking in the shop windows, the glass figurines inside garish and dappled, some green like the convent nursery's walls.

I slept with the slim volume of Allegra's letters underneath my mattress, though I did not read them, could not look at the name she'd learned to write herself, the cumbersome capital *A*.

I never lay down unless I was sure I was too tired to think, too worn down to remember. When I didn't sleep, she came to me, young and alive, olives in her mouth, the child I knew better than my own. Their eyes and fingers became the same in my dreams.

Lucia Joyce dancing in Paris at the Bullier Ball, May 1929. **Photo reprinted with permission of the Stuart Gilbert Collection at the Harry Ransom Center, University of Texas, Austin.**

EXPRESSION THEORY

L drinks from a broken teacup and splits her lip. She doesn't wipe the blood with a napkin but sucks it away, glaring up at her mother with crooked eyes.

I don't take pleasure in summer eggs, L says.

Why do you speak in irregular sentences? her mother asks.

I have no native tongue, L says. What do you expect?

There's a chamber pot on the couch and the house smells terrible in the heat. A boiled egg sits on the plate in front of her; L cuts it open but doesn't eat. This offends her mother, she can tell. She knows what her mother is thinking: These eggs cost money.

L is choreographing in her head again, making mental diagrams: the arch of a back, a lunge, a flexed foot. Her own bare feet tap the floor of the rented flat. She wants to stumble upon an invisible idea and render it with her body, amplify it. She feels something savage and raw inside and wants to show it on the stage, or in a patron's garden. She wants to begin a discussion underneath the orange trees.

Lucia, her mother says, leaning on the counter in her outdated, coffee-stained couture. You need to empty the pot.

I'm working.

Nonsense.

L's imagination is back in Antibes. She bathes in the Baie des Anges and dances in the woods with unshowered, muscular girls in tunics, loose hair tumbling down their backs. They give nighttime shows, the flicker of oil lamps on their damp skin. Her muscles were firmer then. She spoke three languages. She was on the verge of something. Her thoughts were the color of moss and her head was teeming with them. The ideas were crawling all over her body like the fat worms she used to feed the rooster after a rain, the lonely one who crowed in the city streets at dawn, the one who sought shelter behind a fetid wastebin.

L, the pot. Remember the pot.

But L remembers the olive grove and the moon. Those are doorways in her imagination. If you have dreamed of something taboo, she thinks, say your brother's tongue, you must not let the image go. You must let it unlock something for you artistically, because it's part of the rhythm. You must let the native tongue torture you slowly, make you ask what in the pit of humanity makes you want to turn away. What does the moral filter look like? What might the arm do? The leg?

She taps her foot.

L, the pot is stinking up the room! Stop tapping.

If you have fingered a rose blossom, she thinks, you know the shape of a clitoris. You picture it between your teeth. You squeeze it with your fingers. How can I make the shape of that feeling? What color is a lunge? What does an arabesque sound like?

Why had she stopped dancing? *Stanchezza? Wahnsinn?* The string of broken engagements? A wounded ego? Last week, when she couldn't answer this question, she went walking. Her mother called it tramping but she went walking, stumbling through the streets with her dark hair unbrushed. She was hungry, almost catatonic, until she found a man she could press up against. A man who would give her bread.

The pot!

L stands up. She grabs a chair and hurls it

at her mother, who shields her face. The chair lands on the floor, leg breaking. How can the body be like the chair? Who is watching? Her life is a performance.

Aggression is ugly in a woman. What color is it?

Last night the man who broke her heart walked into her father's birthday party as if it was nothing. As if her body had meant nothing to him. As if she had given him nothing. She was once a silver fish, her body swallowed in a costume of scales. He had been in the audience, watching.

What if I bastardized a grand plié, assumed the position of birth, squatted down like a woman in the Amazon? L thinks as her mother sobs. Would that look useful?

L retreats to her room. Her walls are painted black and they smell like the woods at night. Her curtains are made of punctured records and they sound like gunfire. She is a tree, and all her leaves are on the ground. She is naked, picked clean. She is a river, barren.

Butterfly McQueen. **Photo reprinted with permission of Mary Evans Picture Library.**

SAVING BUTTERFLY McQUEEN

Before we slice the cadavers open, a Unitarian chaplain offers a prayer. It's a hot August day in Baltimore. The breeze stirs the magnolia trees outside the lab window; the leaves scratch the glass and block the sun, leaving a mottled pool of light beneath our gurneys.

"We're grateful for these gifts," the chaplain says. "May the bodies of these men and women provide the light of truth and help you practice better medicine."

"Break out the bone saws!" one of my classmates calls out. We are, I think, eager to show mettle we don't yet have. The jokes are a coping mechanism; you earn your indifference to blood and guts. Each of us is anxious to unzip the body bag and see who we will disembowel in the name of science.

Our instructor is clear that we shouldn't name our cadaver, but of course we do. Our cadaver is fat, and has thick black chest hair.

We call him Vegas. My lab partner, Sarah, slides a pair of cheap aviator sunglasses over his pale, waxen nose.

"As long as I can't see his eyes, I'm fine," she says.

"We have to flip him over first anyway," I say, slipping my fingers underneath his buttocks to get a sense of his weight.

"God," I say. "He's big." And full of embalming fluid.

"I thought they stopped taking the fat ones," Sarah says. "Maybe there was a shortage?"

"Maybe," I say, though the lab tech told me the school morgue has more bodies than it can handle; the economy is bad and the costs of burial are up.

"Old Vegas smells like toilet cleaner," Sarah says. "Or menthol cigarettes."

Sarah is hardly five feet tall and tenacious in the way of a terrier. Her parents are internists in Ohio, and I get the feeling that she's impatient about school. "I'm ready to marry myself to the hospital halls," she says, "or the first anesthesiologist that looks like *Top Gun*-era Val Kilmer."

"Goggles are a must when sawing bone," our lab instructor tells us. "Watch out for bionic knees and hips; the metal will take out your eye."

We come to the gurney well aware of the risks: the scent of phenol may make us salivate and become strangely hungry. We may not want meat for months.

Sarah makes a point of discussing her craving for beef carpaccio. "I like a little blood on my plate," she says.

"Who are you?" I ask.

"It's his heart that did him in," Sarah says, aiming her scalpel at his bare chest. "Blockage. I know it. I can't wait to get in there."

With the help of our group members, we flip Vegas onto his stomach. Touching his body gives me chills. Surely this is not what he wanted, students making fat jokes and speculating about his cause of death. Though I'm determined to remain exceedingly rational during med school, part of me wonders if some piece of Vegas's soul is aware of what we're doing to him. What would he say to us, if he could?

I run my scalpel down his vertebrae, not cutting, just thinking, and know I should be focused, the surgical scissors not quite a familiar weight in my hand. Grabbing on to his hip with the ferocity of a lover, I'm about to go wrist-deep, slice through subcutaneous fat, peel the skin off Vegas's back like a rug, when my thoughts turn to Butterfly McQueen.

■ ■ ■ ■

In the winter of 1994 I carried a Bible around a historic neighborhood in Augusta, Georgia, evangelizing in the name of love. We had a new youth minister, a fresh graduate from Duke Divinity School. Lank Harris. He was blond, dimpled, and his father owned a car dealership in town.

Lank had what he called a ministry project, a postgraduate demonstration of ideas in action. "Roughly one-third of our neighborhood is Christian," he told us one Sunday, "but most of them are elderly. Think about it — we only have a short while to lead the other two-thirds to God."

I was vain and ambitious in those days, and easily moved. I've always had get-an-A syndrome, so when Lank casually mentioned he could use some volunteers for his ministry project, I blushed, raised my hand, and said I was available. He nodded approvingly in my direction. The Sunday evening light came in blue through the stained glass, and I felt hot inside with righteousness, or perhaps an early notion of lust.

My eyes never left Lank during youth group. He sat in the middle of a semicircle of folding chairs, Bible on his knee. I stared at his bare, tan ankles; like most of the men at Heyside Baptist, he wore his loafers without socks. The skin, exposed when he crossed his legs and his pressed khakis rose up his leg, fascinated me with its adult qualities. Though he would turn out to be someone I was embarrassed to smile at when I returned home from college, he was my first crush. After youth group I practiced French kissing Lank, sliding my tongue across the bathroom mirror, full of wonderment and a little shame.

The Sunday afternoon of my short-lived evangelical career, I arrived in white shorts my mother and I had argued over. The crepe myrtles dumped pink petals onto the parking lot, browned by the morning's fast rain and the wheels of Mom's Chrysler minivan.

"You're going to lead people to the Lord in booty shorts?" Mom had said.

Though I didn't see it then, she was always calling me to reason, nudging me to laugh at the world. Or myself. She had some brains behind her suntan, but she spent her prime shuttling me between school and the softball field, between a split-level home and extracurricular activities in which I did not excel. She liked Agatha Christie and Mary Kay, chose the Junior League over college.

She rented out our home every year for the big golf tournament, cleaning the place frantically for the caddies and their families, decking it out with bouquets of lilies and her grandmother's china, earning enough to pay my undergraduate tuition in cash.

Three of us from youth group showed up that day, all girls in short hemlines, all ready to lead the elderly to the Lord for the love of Lank Harris. After flirting with our mothers — or maybe it was the other way around — he led us across the road and into the neighborhood he had in mind, four blocks of Sears kit bungalows, shotgun shacks, and the occasional vinyl-sided contemporary cape.

"Who wants the hard one?" he said, turning to us beneath an ancient oak tree.

We all raised our hands. The humidity plastered my hair to my forehead and the back of my neck. Sunlight glinted off the long blond leg hairs I'd missed shaving.

"Anyone know Butterfly McQueen?" Lank asked.

None of us did. He told us she was a former actress and an avowed atheist. We nodded and made knowing, sad eyes at each other. "What movies?" we asked.

"*Gone With the Wind*," Lank said. "She was one of the maids, the one that said 'I don't know nothin' bout birthin' babies!' But don't ask her about the movie."

"Why?" we asked.

"She doesn't like to talk about it. She thinks her role reinforced stereotypes."

I nodded as if I understood, but Mom had not yet let me watch the movie. Living in the South, one could know the movie without ever having seen it. Mom's bridge group had *GWTW* parties, gatherings that included hats, gloves, mint juleps, and red velvet cakes. These women named their cats Scarlett and Rhett, had homes that looked like the Kmart version of Tara, and took it personally that the burning of Atlanta had been filmed not in Georgia but in Hollywood. In 1939, war raging, my grandmother and her sister had dressed in period clothing and waited six hours on Peachtree Street in Atlanta to watch Vivien Leigh's motorcade drive by. Decades later, leafing through the scrapbook with stars in her eyes, she told me about the ovations for Confederate veterans, the chilly air shot through with roving spotlights.

"We've been working Prissy for years," Lank said, using her character's name. "What I want you to do is think of Jeremiah 20:9. *His word is in my heart like a fire, a fire shut up in my bones.* Can you feel that?"

We nodded again.

"I said can you *feel* that?"

"Yes." YES.

"Elizabeth," Lank said, looking me deep in the eyes. "I want you to go in there and say everything we've practiced. I want you to ask Butterfly to let the light of the Lord into her heart."

"I will," I said, on fire not for the Lord but for Lank Harris.

"No one has ever been able to get through to her," he whispered. "That's how I'll know I have a star on my hands."

Lank abandoned me at her door, which was flanked with a broom, parched flowers, and a pair of small tennis shoes. I took a deep breath, rang the bell, and stepped back from the door. Nothing.

"Ring again," Lank mouthed from the sidewalk, gesturing with his finger before heading down the block. He didn't go far. I suspected only later that he liked to watch people struggle.

The door opened slightly, and Butterfly put her head through the crack. She was a small woman, and we stared at each other eye to eye. I was surprised at the immediate feeling of embarrassment that washed over me. I was starstruck, nauseated. She was famous and I wasn't. She was part of one of the South's biggest cultural moments. She had touched Vivien Leigh.

"What do you want, honey?" she asked. Her voice was high-pitched and childlike even though she was in her eighties. She wore her white hair pulled back and smiled apprehensively. The crack of the door widened.

"I want to talk to you about your faith," I said, using the line I had practiced with Lank.

Butterfly scoffed. "Again? You can tell that minister of yours that he can stop trying," she said. "Don't you think everyone else has already tried? My family? My friends?"

"He cares for you," I said.

"Who?"

"The Lord," I said.

"I won't be anyone's trophy," she said, pointing to her head. "I can think on my own."

I took a deep breath. I started to wonder if I had the guts, maybe even the faith, to see this through. I searched in my heart for some deeper commitment, some understanding about the universe that I had and Prissy didn't, but I came up empty.

"If you believe in your heart that Jesus is Lord and that God raised him from the dead —"

"I don't believe any of that," she said, "and I got tired of pretending. Aren't you?"

I said nothing. All I had were canned lines, which I had memorized dutifully but could not — when it counted — feel or defend.

"Trust me — I'm trying to do right by others and be honest at the same time," she said.

"Don't you worry about what's going to happen when you die?" I said, suddenly genuinely curious.

"I already know what's going to happen when I pass," she said. "I'm giving my body to science."

I was dumbfounded.

"To do some real good," she said. "Good we can see and good we can know."

I forgot about the Lord. "What will they do with your body?"

"Cut it open, learn, give my organs to someone who needs them," she said. "I don't know and I don't care."

This was the first time I'd ever heard of someone not wanting to lie in a grave in their best dress, plastic lilies stuck in the ground next to a granite tombstone. It seemed to me so rational and selfless, one of the greatest gifts you could give: your whole body.

"Now if you'll excuse me —"

"I was hoping —"

"I know you were, but I'm going to save your time," she said. "Go on to the next house, honey."

The door shut and I stood there looking at it, stunned.

"And God bless," Lank whispered from behind an azalea bush, whose blooms had withered and were now brown and plastered to the porch.

"Say it," he hissed.

"And God bless," I said, my voice anemic.

"Next house up," Lank said, wiping sweat from his brow. "Keep momentum."

"I want to call my mom," I said, tugging at the hemline of my shorts.

"You're letting fear in," Lank said, holding me by the elbow. He craned over me, eyes earnest, skin tanned from frequent golf games.

But what I'd really let in was a kernel of doubt.

Butterfly's black cat stared at me through the window, ambivalent. "I want to go home," I said.

I didn't think of Butterfly again for years, not until I was twenty-four years old and in bed with my mother, watching *Gone With the Wind*.

Those days I was working a job as a marketer at a firm in Richmond, *marketer* meaning someone who scheduled conference calls and hounded executives for calendar time nine hours a day. I'd married the wrong guy, and too young. I ate everything put in front of me. Anytime I got into my car alone, I cried. Two decades into life and I was burnt out.

Mom was in and out of sleep that day, exhausted from radiation treatments. I held her hand and ate two doughnuts and an entire bag of popcorn. At that time in my life, movies were salvation. I could quiet my brain, stop thinking about the things I didn't understand: my mother's cancer, pharmacology, why I didn't love my perfectly nice husband. Instead I could marvel at Vivien Leigh's waistline, her savage femininity.

But then Scarlett, outraged with Prissy's failure to find a doctor when Melanie was in the throes of labor, shoved her on the staircase. I froze.

"Oh my God," I said, sitting up. I was struck by how horrendous that scene was, how sharp. No wonder Butterfly was uncomfortable with her role.

"That's how it was," Mom said, stirring. I brought her broth.

Three weeks later she was dead. Lank spoke at her service, his blond hair now thinned out on top and swept to the side, but I was too ripped open by grief to listen. I'd tuned him out years ago.

It turns out that Vegas had cancer, and this sobers us. One of our team members finds a chemotherapy port surrounded by puckered skin and scar tissue.

"I can't believe I was wrong about his heart," Sarah says.

"You could still be right," I say. "We'll know in a few weeks."

While we wait for the lab technician to inspect our work, Sarah tells me that she'd like to open a free clinic in Florida for the workers who get bused in for orange picking. "They have these makeshift camps," Sarah says. "And no health care. What about you?"

"What about me?" I ask.

"Why did you come here?"

"After my mother died," I say, "I quit my marketing job and started taking biology classes at the community college."

"So you didn't always want to be a doctor?" she asks, as if this is a strike against my character.

"No," I say. "Definitely not."

"What do you think Vegas did before he died?" she asks. "Landscape architect? Toll booth operator? Who *are* these people?"

That night, as I scrub the embalming fluid from my hands — it had seeped into my gloves and made my fingers tingle — I remember how Butterfly McQueen died.

Mom read the obituary to me at the kitchen table. I was in high school, fifteen or so, and constantly sulking, but the news had caught my attention. It had been a little over a year since I'd met Butterfly, and she'd lodged in my imagination. She'd been a dancer, a maid, a Harlem social worker, and attended college in her sixties. I recall something she said in an interview about how she wouldn't let Vivien Leigh slap her, and refused to eat watermelon. I remember cringing at the sound of her roles: maid, Auntie, a "blind negress" in *Huckleberry Finn*.

Butterfly died horrifically, burned from a kerosene heater she tried to light. I picture her leaning toward the small heater in the living room of her Georgia home, trying to take the chill out of the December air, then shrieking and pulling back as the flames burst up and onto her small body. Did someone find her before she died? How long did she lay there burning?

I do my best to imagine her body, her suffering, and how I would have treated her wounds. Cooling. Pain management. Fluids — lactated Ringer's maybe?

But with Butterfly it wasn't just about treating a physical ailment. Her body was more than burned flesh. Donating it to science was about taking control of the thing that was undeniably hers. Had that chance been taken from her? There were only so many ways to show the world that she was more than a petite maid cowering on the stairs underneath Vivien Leigh's raised palm.

Were doctors able to use her body as she wanted? The epidermis would have been too damaged for lab work. Maybe her organs, though old, were still helpful to someone.

I find myself hoping that her wish was granted, that her body found the purposeful end she'd imagined.

But I know so little. I still catch myself looking away when a slide comes up of necrotic tissue or reveals the yellow tint of a swollen limb. A burned body — it's only a matter of time before I see one.

It is, I'm learning, weird to get close to a body in decline. The qualities we are afraid to discover in ourselves, or others, are pushed to the front.

My mother's was the first dead body I knew, the first one I touched. I gripped the hand that had masterfully applied Mary Kay eye shadow, lipstick, and mascara. The hand that had braided my hair, slapped my cheek, and held me to her breast when I was an infant. She wanted a wig and the mortician's makeup for the casket. I didn't pass along her wishes. Does it matter what we do when consciousness has passed? I was the one who had to look at her, and I wanted the real her, even if the real her was hairless and wasted.

Years from now there will be bodies I have loved and bodies I have treated. After a few weeks with Vegas, I'm sure my compassion toward the dying will be tinged with scientific intrigue, a desire to understand and solve problems.

What I know now: the body is a strange vessel we leave behind.

Sarah is anxious about her cutting skills. "I think I'm too excited," she says. "I'm going too deep."

We all have performance anxiety, but that's not what keeps me up at night. Me — I'm afraid I'll become one of those doctors who sees a patient and not a person, the body and not the spirit.

What I hope, I guess, is that the right kind of callus will form around my heart.

The upperclassmen tell us we will struggle most not with intestines or livers but with the cadaver's hands, genitals, and face — the things we see as inextricably human.

It's my turn to make an incision on Vegas's back as we search for the trapezius muscle. *You will always remember the first cut.* I look for the part of myself who can detach from her surroundings and find that she is there, all business, working for the A.

The scalpel is sharper than I imagined and the skin gives way easily. I will know what Vegas never could, the thickness of his muscles, the color of his subcutaneous fat. I bend over, get closer. The bright light spares nothing.

Dolly Wilde, photographed by Cecil Beaton. **Photo reprinted with permission of Sotheby's.**

WHO KILLED DOLLY WILDE?

You wouldn't have liked Dolly if you met her, that last year. She spent a lot of time screaming in her bedroom, complaining about the wallpaper. She claimed she couldn't be left alone with bad wallpaper, because that was how her uncle Oscar had died, and she was his reincarnation, and wasn't it dangerous to leave a narrative thread dangling that way?

"Isn't it just asking for trouble?" she'd ask me, rolling over in her bed, naked. She'd been athletic as a young girl, but looking at her pale legs, I realized her muscles had gone soft in middle age. Sometimes she wore silk pajamas peppered with cigarette burns, but she was often naked. She was ashamed of her negligible bank account and empty bottle of Guerlain — never her body, not even the track marks on her arms.

I knew Dolly wanted to go back to the Hotel Montalembert in Paris, but she'd

227

been kicked out of the hotel at least twice and it was impossible to get into Paris now with the war. She kept bad company, odd hours, and rarely paid her bills. She'd drink an expensive bottle of champagne and take the warm dregs of the bottle with her to the kitchen and smoke cigarettes with the line cooks in the back alley. Her fluidity attracted people to her as a young woman — she knew how to cultivate obsession — but now her intensity made people uncomfortable. She wanted things: conversation, money, drugs, a hot meal, sex. She wore the want on her face; I could see it in her violet eyes every time she looked at me.

"No more bacon in bed," she complained. "No more love letters on expensive hotel stationery."

"You aren't allowed back there," I'd say, shrugging my shoulders. "And besides you have this smart flat that's all yours." She lived on Chesham Street near Belgrave Square, a small place with a posh address and a crummy interior that was also close to the physicians' offices she tore through on Sloane Street.

"It's so bleak in here," she said, sighing. "The lighting is bad, and the maid mumbles . . ."

"She's intimidated by you," I said, but the

right word would have been *horrified,* because the young woman had happened
upon Dolly in various states of undress,
wretched hangovers, and what might have
been described as fits of madness, usually
brought on by the sirens that wailed
throughout London in the evenings. Dolly
had to dope herself to sleep every night as
the Luftwaffe bombed London into blocks
of fire, making hollowed-out silhouettes of
old buildings.

I think she saw her life as it was: over. As
the war and her cancer progressed, I
watched her try to decide if she wanted to
end it all or resurrect herself, rejoin the
intellectual set, make things right with the
people who had once loved her but now
ceased to answer her desperate letters.

Dolly was often high, out of her mind
nearly half of the day. I don't know where
she got the drugs, but she always had them.
Paraldehyde, heroin, morphine — she was
indiscriminate. But despite the relentless
ways she poisoned herself, she would obsess
over what brand of deodorant or toothpaste
to use, panic over small rashes and coughs,
and phone me multiple times a day to
discuss her ailments.

"I've noticed a spot underneath my armpit
and must go to the physician's at once,"

she'd say. "You'll take me, darling, won't you?"

I would.

I loved Dolly in the way that you can only love your first love, a way that is infinitely forgiving and always mindful of the early days. We'd been friends since we were children. I used to give Dolly my nice dresses because I had no place to wear them; I hated parties. I knew she'd never return them and if she did they'd be wrinkled and stained.

I had to be patient — I couldn't abandon her — she was a dying woman, in many ways. There was the cancer, of course, but also the sort of dying that happens when the beautiful person you once were wears off and all that's left is someone frightened and ugly, this hard and cruel kernel of a self that's difficult to look at.

If you can love her through this part, I told myself, you *are* the love of her wild and miserable life.

Nearly every day I walked through the smoking rubble of London, past the crippled chimneys and grieving mothers, past the men blacking out the lights along the Thames, past the people going to work, and I knocked on the door of Dolly's flat to see if she was okay. It was part of my wartime routine. We all had them, the things you did to reassure yourself that you were still alive.

You're a good person, I told myself. You're her only friend.

Every afternoon she ate fish soup at Russo's, and sometimes I joined her. She wore the same blue dress over and over again, because she thought she looked good in it or maybe it was the last designer dress she had. Dolly would rather be caught twice in the same well-made dress than wear something cheap.

She rubbed her shoulders. I looked at the toile tablecloths, worn from bleaching. There were anemic flowers on the round bistro tables. A little winter sun came through the wide windows.

"Where's your coat?" I asked.

She didn't answer.

"Tell me."

"I pawned it," she said, staring me right in the eyes, daring me to judge her. I sighed.

Dolly swallowed the fish soup, wincing a little at its heat. "It makes me think of drowning in the ocean," she said, letting her spoon rest in the bowl for a moment. "Of getting knocked down by a wave and coming up with shells pressed to your knees, the inside of your nose stinging with salt. Do you remember that feeling?"

I nodded.

The soup was thin, and I think eating it was an act of contrition for her. I took a few polite bites; I'd eat at home later. We still had a cook and black market food, and I knew how lucky that made me.

"I don't have much of an appetite," Dolly confessed, swirling the soup. "But last week I spent the last of my monthly allowance on a hunk of Camembert and a buttery brioche. I pulled the knob off the top of the pastry and left the rest at the boulangerie," she said, one side of her mouth twisted into a half smile.

"Why didn't you wrap it in a napkin and save it for later?" I asked. She didn't answer; I knew she resented my veiled attempts at financial advice. She was prone to spontaneous, wasteful gestures. I think they made her feel luxurious.

I missed her better stories, the days when she might hold forth about listening to George Antheil's *Ballet Mécanique* in a private garden, eating figs in Algiers, a sheikh kissing her stockinged leg. There was opium shared with Cocteau behind heavy velvet curtains in a private club she could never find on her own. I needed these stories because I had none of my own. I was too wealthy to work — my mother forbade it — and too shy to have my own adventures. After finishing school — Dolly liked to ask "finished for what?" — I read books, kept my mother company at teatime, and lived vicariously through Dolly. It had always been that way; it was our currency.

"Something sweet?" the waiter asked.

We shook our heads, and he left with a smile that was focused on Dolly.

"He's Parisian," she explained, rifling through her wallet. "He says my French is impeccable, and for that he gives me a half carafe of wine some nights."

She placed a few coins on the white tablecloth.

Je suis désolée, she said to the waiter. I'll come back with a tip. *Ne vous inquiétez pas,* he said, his thin face expressing something like sympathy. He poured more water into her glass and went back to the kitchen.

"I look like someone you should be nice to now," Dolly mumbled. "Not someone you want to sleep with."

I put more coins on the table and walked her back to her flat.

"I heard on the wireless that you have a one in ten thousand chance of dying each night in a raid," I said, thinking those chances sounded pretty favorable.

"My chances are much better," Dolly said, squeezing my hand.

In reality she was probably more likely to die of an overdose than in a raid. The paraldehyde vials were everywhere in her room, giving it a distinct vinegary smell.

I knew Dolly wanted desperately to believe in her own glamour and bravery — twenty years ago she *had* been brave, a volunteer ambulance driver on the front lines of the First War, dodging bombs and changing her own tires under the spray of bullets — but we both knew that instead of making love to androgynous heiresses and sticking it to the Germans, she was now lying comatose in her bed, racked by hallucinations.

When we were younger I'd envied Dolly's worldliness and experience to the point of pain; it made me feel weak, pampered, and inadequate. While my brother and Dolly were off fighting, I went with my mother to the cathedral to assemble care packages of Bovril and cigarettes for soldiers. I slept in a soft bed my entire life. I've never seen a dead body, let alone thousands.

"Would you stay with me?" Dolly asked. "We can read the paper and I can make you some tea."

"I guess I could stay for a little while," I

said. "But I can't miss my train."

"I'll braid your hair," she said, pulling me closer. "The way I used to."

I'd never had any boyfriends to speak of. I liked to be touched and she knew it.

"How's your mum?" she asked.

"The nights are hard for her," I said. "Even out in the country. We can still hear the planes."

"I cry myself to sleep every night," Dolly said, staring at the street. "The sounds, the vibrations. It's too much."

Yes, Dolly had once been a hero.

Now she was just a coward and we both knew it.

How had Dolly first come to our house? I can't remember, but it must have been because of my mother, who was a collector of Oscar's manuscripts and clothes. She owned two of his dress shirts, a handful of personal letters, early notes for *Dorian Gray,* and pamphlets from his lecture series, and kept them in a trunk in her room. Over time I've come to believe my obsession with Dolly was first hers. My mother, a bored and wealthy housewife, heard of Oscar's brother's poverty and helped pay the bills for Dolly's birth in a pauper's ward. Over the years she bought artifact after artifact and kept Dolly's mother afloat.

Mum's money hadn't kept Dolly out of a convent, where she'd been tossed for a while as a child, but she came back to us as an adolescent with some obligation toward my mother that she wanted to honor. She joined us for dinner weekly, and we all fell in love with her in our different ways. My mother loved her resemblance to Oscar. I loved the way she recited Byron, and the way she made me feel. She disarmed my shyness in a way no one else ever had, coaxed words and laughter out of me, forced me into stating my opinions — *but how do you really feel about long underwear?* — snuck D. H. Lawrence books into my room and left them underneath my silk pillowcase. She knew my insecurities and had once, well into a bottle of wine, recited them: "men, your hawk-like nose, your lack of success as a painter, your knobby knees, and your boring existence supported by your family and not yourself."

Dolly was the exclamation point in my life. She made me feel things: adoration, anger, frustration. She was always in love and it made her glow.

But she didn't glow anymore.

The following day I was sitting on the edge of her bed as she slept. We were supposed to go out for tea and then volunteer at the cathedral making care packages for soldiers, but she was in no shape to leave her flat. I knew tears would stream down her face in the afternoon sun; her pale eyes were sensitive to light. Her sheets were damp; she suffered from night sweats. I let her sleep.

I saw a small packet of letters tied with blue silk ribbon on her bedside table, right next to two vials of what must have been paraldehyde. The letters' edges were tattered. Curiosity seized me. I knew deep down I shouldn't read them, that even the most boisterous, immodest people have secrets and a need for privacy, but I wanted to believe — I have *always* wanted to believe — that I'm Dolly's sister, or something more, maybe an extension of her, and therefore it would be okay if I merely peeked at a letter or two.

For years people who admired Dolly's wit and entertaining personal letters pleaded with her to write a book, but she never had. She was lazy, but I think she was also stymied by her uncle's shadow.

"How can I be any good if he has used it all up?" she once said to me.

When I opened the first letter I found pages of her looping script; I knew it like

my own. I was surprised to see it was a letter to a girl named Betty Carstairs, a girl
she called Joe. I felt a pang of jealousy, just
as I had when Dolly came home and talked
ceaselessly about how fast Joe could change
a tire, how she cut her hair like a man —
the type of women Dolly loved were women
I could never be.

It's not a dream if it really happened, it's a
memory that comes to me in my sleep, isn't
it? Do you have these same nightmares?

I'm driving my ambulance over the war-
scorched earth, toward the front lines in Verdun. It's March 1916, and you would have
been out doing the same. The ground is black,
and covered in piles of receding snow. Naked
trees jut from the earth. The Meuse River is
an ice slick, its banks covered in unexploded
shells, split limbs. I pass the white-rubble ruins
of all those nameless villages, approaching
Fort Souville from the south. Where farms,
churches, and green fields once stood lie piles
of German stick grenades, bomb scars, and
dead bodies. My wheels shake and skid over
potholes. I grip the steering wheel so hard my
frozen knuckles bleed.

In this dream, and maybe you have some
like it, I haven't slept for thirty-two hours. I
can't feel my fingers, nose, or ears. I've long
since forgotten to be hungry.

238

As I get closer to Fort Souville, I can see smoke — or is it fog? — rising from the gouged hills. My windshield is cracked and my jacket is ripped. Everything in me wants to turn around, but I can't. It's my duty to continue; this is why I ran away from home; this is the adventure I wanted. I thought I wanted. Dolly Wilde, ambulance driver. Dolly Wilde, patriot. Dolly Wilde, adventuress. And we did have adventures, didn't we? Valid adventures. But we paid for them, you and I.

In the dream I can never turn back, and I wake up sick with dread, because I don't know if I could still do the things that we did then, see the things that we saw. We were just children, weren't we? Young girls who were going to do their part?

I thought that life as an ambulance driver — wrapping broken limbs, plucking lice from my hair, kicking ice from the wheels — was the antithesis of pleasure seeking, the only way I could avoid repeating my uncle's flawed existence. Everyone told me I had his face. Even you said, "It is Oscar incarnate, only much prettier . . ."

What we saw changed me. Those days are why I don't cry at weddings, why I drink, why I say something rash at dinner. They are why I forget to pay my bills. They are why I can't sleep. They are what I see in my sleep. They are why I don't waste time doing practical things, hoping the world will be good to me when I'm older. Tell me, Joe, do you think the world is still good to women like us? To anyone?

How are your boats? I miss driving. If only I had a car of my own.

You said in your last letter that I taught you flexible thinking, but I don't think anyone can teach you much. As for my writing, I have nothing to show. The world prefers listening to me, looking. That's what I was made for I suppose.

When Dolly began to stir I slowly tucked the stack of letters into my leather bag. She would miss it, of course, but given how much of her life she spent blacked out, she'd assume it was misplaced, knocked behind the bureau.

"How long have you been here?" she asked, licking her lips, stretching her arms. She looked old.

"Only a minute. I'll let you rest," I said. I kissed her cheek and let myself out of the flat. I walked to the train, aware that the light was fading and night was coming on soon. The city seemed heavy, mid-sigh, as if bracing itself for a blow, and I guess it was.

On the train back home to my mother's empty mansion in the countryside — I

never thought of it as mine, I had nothing
— I dozed off, then woke up in a semilucid
state. I closed my eyes again and saw Dolly
in her prime.

She was descending a staircase slowly,
dressed as her uncle Oscar in a borrowed
fur coat. A hush came over the crowded
foyer — how many women can silence a
crowd? Dolly could.

The cane Dolly carried clicked on every
stair. She thrust her chin into the air and
then looked down, making eye contact with
the people beneath her. She remained in
character, though it wasn't much of a
stretch; Dolly was gregarious at parties and
depressed the morning after. But she had
dressed to awe us and she did; she made
the papers the next day: *Niece Dolly Brings
Oscar Back to Life.*

And though I was fascinated by her, I
hated seeing her like this, drinking up her
own social success. Her laugh reached
across the room and strangled me. No, I
preferred private Dolly. I liked Dolly in my
library with a book on her lap, not perched
on the arm of a plush sofa with champagne
in hand, someone, anyone, kissing her neck.

I left the party early that night.

I always left parties early.

■ ■ ■ ■

A week later I went to meet Dolly at Russo's and was disappointed to see her friend Jeanette there. She and Dolly were over-dressed for the venue, but they both had more panache than money, a quality in a woman that bothered my mother, and I guess it bothered me too.

Jeanette wore a fox stole and tapped her nails on her water glass as I approached. She shifted in her chair. She was bird-thin and just past pretty, her blond hair going gray, her gray eyes blinking repeatedly. She lit a cigarette, looking at her fingers as if she was impatient with their inability to move faster with the match. She brought the small fire to her face.

"Good afternoon," I said.

"Let's get another chair," Dolly said apologetically, waving to the waiter, her waiter.

"Welcome," Jeanette said, exhaling. Her voice was pitchy and plaintive.

She and Dolly had been friends for years now. They'd met over an opium pipe at Le Boeuf sur le Toit.

"I love meeting people that way," Dolly had once confided in me. "Colliding into them. There's a strange intimacy that comes with intoxicated conversations. You discard barriers. You're interesting and filled with a peculiar energy, and you just want to share it."

"I wouldn't know," I'd said.

Dolly had nodded and patted my thigh in a way that was both insulting and compassionate.

The waiter brought the third chair and we sipped water in silence. Jeanette muttered something awful about "death and destruction becoming monotonous," and Dolly rose from the table.

"Excuse me," she said. "I'm going to the ladies' room."

"Here," Jeanette said, fishing around inside her worn leather handbag to produce a monogrammed silver compact. "Take this."

I knew it was packed with cocaine. I also knew Jeanette thought I was naïve. These situations were common in Dolly's company and used to make me feel insecure. Now I just felt infuriated, fatigued.

Dolly placed the compact into her own bag and walked through the restaurant with feigned elegance. Whenever I watched her walk in public I remembered a line someone had written anonymously about her during a Victorian parlor game called Honesty: *Dolly doesn't walk, she lumbers.*

Dolly had cried to me that night. "They used to call Uncle Oscar elephantine. I'm the same way. I'm not built like a woman."

I knew she'd made efforts to shorten her stride and straighten her shoulders. I still felt anger toward whoever had written such a cruel sentence, the kind of sentence that stays with a woman.

I followed Dolly to the small bathroom, which smelled strongly of bleach. The white plaster walls were chipped, and blue curtains framed one small window. Dolly stood in front of the sink blotting her armpits with paper, then her face.

"The cancer makes me sweat more," she said, wrinkling her nose, sniffing.

"I know what's in that compact," I said, standing behind her.

Dolly didn't say anything, but shrugged her shoulders and resumed blotting her face in the mirror.

I returned to the table and sat with my arms crossed. Dolly had a way of making me feel like a petulant child.

"I'm short on cash," Jeanette said, rifling through her leather purse.

"I'll cover you," Dolly said, sitting down. I could tell she was impatient to get home and away from my judgment, maybe away from Jeanette's bony and depressed face. But while she hated to suffer through inconvenient social situations, she also hated being alone.

Dolly's black book — I'd looked through it before — contained contact information for one-night stands, theater boys, dealers, doctors, fake doctors, nurses, ex-girlfriends, aristocrats, art thieves, sodomites, artists, race car drivers, actresses, writers, amateur philosophers, politicians, soldiers, house-wives. She wasn't picky, not these days. She just wanted company, or maybe drugs. She went to parties in abandoned underground stations and on rooftops and God knows where else.

We said good-bye to Jeanette and walked to Dolly's flat in silence.

"It amazes me," she said as we reached her front door, "that you still find the energy to be disappointed in me."

"I'm not disappointed," I said, clutching her hand. "I'm worried."

"I'm late with rent again."

I took a few bills from my purse — half of my monthly allowance — and pressed them into her hand. I had never been good at tell-ing her no, and I wanted to be useful — to anyone, but especially to Dolly. Decades into our relationship, helping her was a reflex.

She kissed the top of my forehead. It was a sisterly gesture.

"Call if you need me," I added.

She nodded and the lock clicked behind her. I headed for the train, aware that after every visit with Dolly I felt exhausted. But these visits were the only breaks in the monotony of my life with Mum, of teas gathered around the wireless, long stretches of reading time, unsatisfactory sessions at my easel.

A few blocks away I heard something moving behind a trash can. Cowering among crates of rotting produce was a brown dog so emaciated I could count her ribs. The dog bared her broken, black teeth and I inched away, wishing I had a few pieces of bread, or anything, to give her.

I hurried into the station.

Safely on the train, I pulled out Dolly's letters and read from them, as I'd developed the habit of doing. This letter was to Natalie, a lover she'd lived with on and off in Paris, and who never had anything to say to me the times I'd visited Dolly in the little garden there.

I hope you'll forgive me for what I said yesterday. I know I've outstayed my welcome, but for Romaine to call me a rat — my temper rose. I'll find a way to repair the vase, darling.

I think, some days, that I'm a broken human being. Last week, the pop of a champagne cork made me sweat. If I stare too long into a fire or smell certain brands of cigarettes and tea, I feel sick, as if the night is coming on in Verdun. Dearest Natalie, please understand — I dream of burned flesh.

Were these drafts of letters, or were they never sent? I folded the papers, carefully tied the ribbon, and stared out of the window. Dolly had a habit of using people like me and Natalie; this was not news. There were years when I convinced myself that she had to rely on others because she was a woman without means who didn't want to marry, and there were years when I got tired of trying to save her, tired of trying to coax her into the incredible woman she should have been. There shouldn't have been flashes of greatness; there should have been a lifetime of it.

A general uneasiness came over me. The train ride was long, cold, and silent.

The next time I came to her door it wouldn't open. The maid had called me.

"I haven't seen Dolly in two days," she said, "but I've heard her and she's howling again, and throwing things at the wall. I think you should come."

"I'll be there tomorrow morning," I said. "Offer her some coffee or even some bread."

Sensing the maid's hesitation, I added, "I'll pay you. Plus a service fee. Just offer her food and drink and let her know that someone cares about her. That part is important."

When I got to Dolly's at ten the next morning, the place was silent. I knocked on the door — nothing. No footsteps, no hello, no swearing. It occurred to me that the inevitable might have happened, that she might have overdosed. I tried my key but couldn't budge the door; she'd pushed something in front of it.

"Dolly!" I screamed, jostling the doorknob, shouting through the small opening. "Let me in."

I pressed my ear to the crack. I heard faint sobbing, then louder cries. I jostled the door some more, but to no avail. At least she was alive.

Because it was a ground-floor apartment, I went around to the outside window and rapped repeatedly.

"Dolly!" I shouted, over and over again. "Let me take you home. Let me take you to the country."

A middle-aged man opened his window and yelled down to me. "Can't you two keep it together? Must you cry and shout so often?"

I glared at him. For the first time I felt as if I had the will to hurt someone. I started to go to the train station, then turned back toward Dolly's flat, feeling as if I'd left something unfinished. I could try harder. I could do more.

I should tell you about her death. No one came to Dolly's funeral but me and two other friends, one who was on crutches. There were fires burning in the city from the evening's raids when she was buried; we could see the smoke and there was, I think, a universal feeling of dread. An urge, maybe, to put Dolly's life and death in context. Did it matter? What was more suffering in a year like this? How many people we knew and loved were dying each day?

The police didn't know the cause of death, and I don't think they cared. Here was an addict who was already dying of cancer; what was her life valued when there were so many children and heroes at risk?

There was a coroner's report, and they asked me to identify the body. I remember looking down at her face in the morgue. It was a large face, moonlike, original except for the fact that it had already been around the block once before as her uncle. Her eyes were closed. I could see the track marks, her brittle hair. Gone was the socialite, the sexpot, the conversationalist. Here was an abused body.

"Goddamnit, Dolly," I said.

At the end, I could no longer pretend she was good, or a valuable member of society. At the end, I could no longer watch what she was becoming. The decline was too disgusting, too steep.

Perhaps the war had made us obsessed with honor and bravery.

Perhaps I became impatient.

When I was younger I wrote her a love letter. I told her that I wanted more from her. That she was beautiful and capable of becoming a great writer and a great human being, and that I could help her if she'd let me. She was twenty-two and just back from the war and I'd missed her so much my stomach hurt and I ran to greet her when she visited the house.

She never responded to the letter, and acted as if she hadn't received it. I was too embarrassed to ask, to force the issue.

Now, reading her letters, I knew more

about the woman I thought I loved. Or maybe I knew less. Maybe what I knew was that there was more mystery and hurt than I could have imagined. Maybe the world had been bad to its great and unusual women. Maybe there wasn't a worthy place for the female hero to live out her golden years, to be celebrated as the men had been celebrated, to take from that celebration what she needed to survive.

And then in the yellowed packet I found an unsent letter addressed to me, from the early days, when she'd first run away to France and I'd lost many nights of sleep worrying about her.

What troubles me about our friendship, darling, is that you live in an alternate universe. You say you want to understand, that you wish you were here with me, so let me tell you about my day:

I back my ambulance into the tent, and jump out of the driver's seat and onto the hard earth, snow to my ankles. I open the rear doors. The putrid smell of gangrene and vomit rushes at me and I dry-heave, covering my mouth with my shoulder. There's no time to clean the ambulance between loads.

It's six a.m., and the shelling has stopped, which means we have a chance to collect bodies. The capable survivors, draped like ghosts in foul wool blankets, hoist the injured out of the dugout with strange efficiency. There are bodies half-lodged in the rubble, arms cocked as if still ready to throw grenades.

I kick my tires to check the air pressure; you don't want to get stuck on the road here, because people die out on the roads. Good tires save lives. My tires are fine, so I wait for orders.

Sixteen, one of the soldiers says, giving me my count. I nod my head, and log the figure with shaking hands in a small black notebook.

Shit, I think.

I will never understand how they decide which bodies are capable of living, but the first one they give me is no longer in human form. The flesh has been burned from his body, what's left of his body. There's no hair, no nose or mouth, just eyes. A face of fire. I could not tell if this man, this body, wished to live, or die.

I hate them for making me see this, for knowing this state of being is possible, for knowing that if I'm in the wrong place at the wrong time and a flame is thrown —

But I hold the soldier's hand — the one he has — and sing to him as I help secure him in the back of my ambulance. I sing "Au Clair de la Lune," and I do not wince, though I am terrified.

Fifteen more are loaded. Trench foot. Lost arm. Legs full of shrapnel.

I climb into the ambulance, start the engine, and pull away from the tent. I can hear a sound more animal than human coming from the back; I know it is the burned one. I drive as fast as I can, the roar of planes overhead, up the icy roads toward camp, knowing he will not be alive when I open the back doors.

Years later, I still imagine how it feels to live inside that body, even for one moment.

I've never heard of women feeling this way. After returning home from the War, am I expected to be beautiful again? I do not feel beautiful inside. I'm expected to respect those who serve, and I continue to tend to soldiers. But who will tend to me when I am home? Will you?

How many times I've seen the eyes of the burned soldier in my sleep. How many times I've tried to look at the world through those eyes. I will never understand what lives are worth saving. I know now I will never understand life, and neither will you.

There is the matter of the last time I saw her, the afternoon when I turned back to her flat. When I threw my weight into the door until my hip was bruised and entered, locking it behind me, displacing the trunk she'd blocked it with, the object I'd had to move with sheer willpower. I barged into her bedroom. She rolled over to look at me, silent and shocked, eyes glazed.

"You're not taking care of yourself," I said, raising my voice. "You're crossing the line."

She groaned and went facedown into her pillow. "Tomorrow," she mumbled, "I'm going to cheer up London's children. The ones hiding in the country."

"You're all talk," I said. "You might have done that when you were younger, but not now. You're wasting your life. You're lazy and troubled and I can't stand it! You have failed yourself!"

"Shut up," she said. "Shut up, shut up, shut up. *Tais-toi!*"

Then she tried to get out of bed, as if she was coming after me, but she collapsed to the floor, first onto her knees and then she was passed out again, sprawled like a corpse.

I dragged her to the bathtub; she was unaware, unhelpful, dead weight. She woke up naked in the cold water and reached out to slap my face.

I slapped her back and it felt good, too good. And then she laughed.

Dolly sang:

The tiny fish enjoy themselves
in the sea.
Quick little splinters of life,
their little lives are fun to them
in the sea!

"D. H. Lawrence, darling!" she said, cocking her head back. Don't you love it? Don't you remember?"

She splashed my face, and I sat fuming. I left her there and began cleaning up bottles, wiping down the bathroom — there was blood.

"Goddamnit, Dolly," I said.

"I need to sleep this off," she interrupted, clumsily reaching for the paraldehyde on the bathroom counter.

"You've already had enough!" She got it down before I could reach her.

— *Jesus Christ!*

And then I let it happen. Because it was the merciful thing to do. I couldn't take it, seeing beautiful Dolly reduced to this.

Killing her was easy; she wanted me to do it. Woman to woman. I'm not even sure she knew who I was, but she offered me her arm and then her thigh. There were needles on the counter.

"More," she said. "More!"

All around me, killers. My brother. My

neighbor. My countrymen. My enemies.

Everyone has a saturation point.

Everyone is capable of radical change. This is what the war has taught me: we kill each other and we kill ourselves. Even though we sleep in nice hotels on soft French linens. Even though we have dresses we never wear. Even though we drink champagne while others work in coal mines or the trenches of Vimy Ridge, smelling of gangrene. We have always been this way, killers inside. It is the human condition.

The world folds in on itself in a ball of fire, and today I walk down Sloane Street, past the small flat near Belgrave Square, the ugly one with the good address. It is part of my wartime routine, how I assure myself I am an ordinary person, and still alive.

And what of it?

Beryl Markham, 1936. **Photo reprinted from the Bibliothèque nationale de France.**

A High-Grade Bitch Sits Down for Lunch

Kenya, 1925

> But this girl, who is to my knowledge very unpleasant and we might even say a high-grade bitch, can write rings around all of us.
> — Ernest Hemingway, on Beryl Markham

The sun was setting over Lake Nakuru, peering through lavender clouds to leave a golden trail across the water.

Beryl leaned against the brick wall of the stable to watch the lake. The horses were munching their hay, and later she'd groom the filly. Or maybe she'd ride the stallion out for the first time, the one she'd gotten for nothing at auction a few weeks ago, the one with the perfect bloodline. The one who'd killed a man with his hooves and teeth in the corner of a stall in Nairobi. If the filly was her favorite, the stallion was her hope.

She ignored his name because she would give him a new one. She'd give him a new life. He would be reborn into glory on the track, and the customers would line up at her door.

Why don't you ride him already? she chided herself. You know you can do it. You'll have to do it if you want to make your money back, and God knows you need money.

Her servant and friend Kibii, whom she'd known all her life, told a client yesterday, "Memsahib is fearless. She's been riding racehorses since she was eleven." True, she'd been raised in Nairobi by a father who raced Thoroughbreds, managed a troubled farm, and forgot her birthday. True, a horse had picked her up in his mouth when she was seven and thrown her; she still had the purple scar on her neck.

She could throw a spear like the Nandi. She could hunt. She rode a half-broken motorcycle over the vacant, muddy road from Nakuru to Nairobi when she got lonely, after dark, when you could hear the lions. Once, when she had to pee, an elephant rose from the dark brush and startled her; she ran back to the motorcycle with her wet pants not entirely up.

"You didn't stand down the elephant?" Kibii asked when she told him, feigning disbelief.

"I'm brave," she said. "Not an imbecile."

She poured herself a glass of wine, measuring it because the bottle had to last a week. A week without guests.

She went back to leaning against the stable. She sipped the wine and watched enormous, salmon-colored clouds of flamingos drag their overturned heads across the muddy shallows of Nakuru. Deafening birdlife meant a constant stream of shit on the racetrack, but her horses were too well trained to stop and smell it, or lick at it the way her dogs did.

I want to be alone when I turn the stallion out, she thought, looking for his proud head over the stall door. I want him to know me as his master, his alpha and omega.

She drank more wine, eyes back on the sunset. She could see the silhouettes of water buffalo grazing by the lake, followed, she knew, by clouds of blackflies and the threat of river blindness. She knew a stable boy who'd poured boiling water down his back to relieve itching caused by the flies. One bite from a fly like that on the stallion's belly and she'd be thrown and broken, left for dead in the ring.

Have I had lunch? she wondered, touching her flat stomach.

No, she had not. Might as well do it now and call it dinner.

Recently divorced and broke, she lived alone in a small white canvas tent underneath the racetrack stands. Her bed was covered in zebra skin. She kept tins of beans next to bottles of wine and boxes of biscuits in a trunk that had once belonged to her father.

She never ate much. Meager eating was good for keeping her figure, and her figure was an asset, on a horse and in the bedroom. She wanted to look good in clothes and out of them.

Cross-legged on the ground, she speared the beans with her fork and took increasingly quick bites.

Today is the day to ride the stallion, she thought, and the light won't last forever.

She stood up and brushed off her legs. She locked up the dogs. She pulled her hair away from her face. She took her riding crop from the corner of the tent.

She'd always been a cruel person, she knew that, and today it was in her favor. Savage practicality and courage had been bred into her, and facing down a beast of a horse in the last hour of light, she could use that.

"Beryl is easily bored," people said. It was true. She was hungry to *feel* something every day, and fear is what she felt pulling open the stall door. She relished the feeling, the goose pimples on her arms, her heightened sense of awareness. Her singular focus.

I will have you, she thought, locking eyes with the regal horse.

The stallion was enormous, seventeen hands high. She could sense the energy he'd built up behind the stall door. She led him to the crossties and put on his tack, carefully, firmly. He swung his head toward her, and she met his face with her elbow. He did it again, and again she met him with her elbow. He balked at the bit and began to pull back, but she waited him out, pressing her thumb into the corner of his mouth, and got it in.

She led him to the ring, careful not to look back, not to show fear. She was the leader and he should follow. She walked the ring, then had him canter, and trot. His muscles excited her. They showed potential. They would make her a winner. Holding on to his lead line, she walked closer to his face.

"Back up," she said.

He didn't. She pressed his broad chest

until he moved. "Back up." She leaned into his back legs to make one cross over the other, the way his mother would have done in the paddock when he was young.

"You're stronger than I am," she said calmly. "But I'm more determined than you. Throw me and I'll get back on. I'll whip you raw."

They could say what they wanted to about her in town. They could say she was a bad wife, too young. They could say she was cruel. She had a stable all to herself in the evenings, and wasn't that better than watching your sad sack of a husband drink himself stupid, fighting him off because you didn't want to sleep with a flaccid, unshowered maniac? Yes. The empty stable was better, even if it meant being unable to buy new clothes. Even if it meant buying your own horses, the dangerous ones you could afford. The ones who'd been passed over, written off.

Don't let your mind wander, she reminded herself. Not even for a second.

She led the stallion to the mounting block. He shifted as she gripped his mane and swung her leg over him. What man would ever be more exciting than this? she thought, squeezing the horse between her strong thighs.

"You will respect me," she said, as he began to turn without her cue. His body stiffened and his head began to dip. He was going to try to throw her, she could feel it.

This battle of wills was real and she would win. She would give herself fully. This moment was falling in love.

At last someone had done something to make them individuals again, they were someone, no longer merely the number tattooed on the arm.

— An extract from the diary of Lieutenant Colonel Mervin Willett Gonin, DSO, who was among the first British soldiers to liberate Bergen-Belsen in 1945

THE INTERNEES

Bergen-Belsen, 1945

We would be famous in an ugly way. We would be black-and-white pictures in textbooks. We would be clavicles and cheekbones and bald heads to learn from.

We could smell the bodies of our own kind.

We were sitting on lice-infested beds when the British soldiers came. The liberators. The heroes that shuttled us through hastily assembled outdoor showers. They hung sheets on the barbed wire to give us privacy, but modesty was something we'd lost. We walked slowly to and from the showers in striped bathrobes, a pattern none of us could look at later in life without pause, without bile rising. Without fear.

They made swings for the children and pushed them into the sky. They deloused us with DDT, spraying it into our hair and underneath our skirts.

We sat next to each other on the floor, covered in sores. Some of us were dying of typhus. Some of us were just dying. Some of us drank water and picked through tin cans of food, though we couldn't eat as much as we wanted. Our bodies couldn't take it. We vomited. We sorted through discarded clothes and disintegrating shoes. We made fires. We looked at the five-digit tattoos on our forearms.

There was a box of expired lipstick that came off the truck. The British soldiers opened the box and threw tubes of lipstick at the crowd, and we wanted it — we were surprised how *badly* we wanted it — and we walked the halls, some of us still without adequate clothing, some of us with piss-drenched blankets tossed over our shoulders like shawls, with scarlet lips. We rubbed the lipstick over our mouths. Over and over. We had pink wax on our rotten teeth. We were human again. We were women.

Everything that makes the world like it is now will be gone.
— Shirley Jackson, "The Lottery"

THE LOTTERY, REDUX

The morning of July 27 was clear to the horizon on all sides of the main island of Timothy, once a large chunk of land but now a series of marshy islets overrun by dragonflies, which moved across town in black, buzzing swarms. The people of Timothy, descendants of men and women exiled from America fifty years ago for crimes against the environment, were gathering by the empty fountain in the square, a place that might have been a village green elsewhere but on Timothy was sand and rock, the brick paths and buildings calcified. The fountain used to flow with seawater, but they'd given up on piping it in. There were more pressing matters, like the afternoon's lottery.

The sounds of morning were the same on any given day: the roar of waves gnawing at the shoreline, the scream of the occasional heron passing overhead, children laughing on the beach, men throwing sandbags or tinkering with the artificial reefs, and Clare Smith leading the women's fishing co-op back from their daily expedition. They walked up from the sea to the picking house, where they broke open crabs with their fingers and skinned fish with rusted bowie knives, gossiping only a little as their eyes were on the fish; they wasted nothing. Today was no exception, and the women were sure to get back on time, as Clare and her fifteen-year-old daughter, June, were in charge of civic duties, including the lottery administration.

The children always followed Clare and the women from the beach up to the picking house to see what the catch looked like, peering into the handwoven baskets at the flopping fish not quite dead and the burlap sacks of freshly dredged oysters. But today the kids — there were only seven of them — were dutifully assembling piles of driftwood on the beach, and mounds of large conchs and shells. Clare, wearing a leather hat with fishhooks slipped over the brim, nodded at them as she and the women walked by. The children waved back to the women, who were still dripping with seawater after braving the rough currents and riptides. They carried spears and rods and threw nets over their browned shoulders like shawls made of old, threadbare lace.

Soon the men began to gather at the dry, chalky fountain, smoking hand-rolled cigarettes, possible because Clare had finally allowed rooftop gardens where people could grow burly, rustic tobacco, which they stuffed into cones of dried seaweed. It was illegal to use pasture space for anything but food crops, but they all agreed the tobacco helped keep things mellow. Now nearly everyone smoked, especially today. Even Summer Hutchison, the seventeen-year-old golden girl of the island, lit a nori cigarette and held it between her teeth as she walked toward the picking house, bucket in hand. She smiled at everyone she passed, licking her dry, chapped lips. She was always cheerful because she was in love, and no one on Timothy was really in love those days. They came to each other's beds because they were bored or obligated, but Summer was in love and the co-op's women agreed it made her pleasant to be around, and so they began to talk about weddings in the picking house, telling stories their mothers had told them about their own weddings, of tossed rice and horse-drawn carriages.

"We could make a veil from an old net," Jade Sleeman said. "We'd drape it like this," she added, gesturing toward her dark cropped hair. Her daughter Lela played underneath the table, stacking empty oyster shells on Jade's toes while the women worked. Jade was thin but strong; her mother had been a horsewoman and a polo player before exile.

Summer smiled. The sun, and there was too much of it, caught in her hair, lit it up like pale stained glass.

"We don't have any nets to spare," Clare said without looking up from the rockfish she was skinning, blade expertly snaking underneath the scaled flesh. When she did look up, gazing out of the window, she could see the men at the fountain, smoking, browned from working all summer long on the artificial reef, which they'd fashioned out of the timbers and iron that washed ashore from a shipwreck they figured sat just east of the island; the pieces tumbled toward them in the strong western current. Though they rarely wore shirts they began pulling them on, and though it was forbidden she knew many of them had stuffed their pockets with gull jerky and marmalade.

But not Javier Lewis, she thought. Javier, hardly twenty, was honorable, and that's why she tolerated this talk of weddings, because he and Summer were the future of

Timothy. They respected tradition and understood what had to be done. She could see Summer looking for him through the big windows, in between feeding empty shells to Lela underneath the table. Clare imagined Summer and Javier with a child. Surely it would be a towheaded baby, kissed constantly, worn on Summer's back as she waded into the water to fish.

"Okay, girls, let's wrap up," Clare said, rising from the wooden table. She plunged the hunks of rockfish into a bucket of brine. As she stood she ducked the emergency rations, salted fish dangling from twine overhead like strange ornaments, drying in the harsh sunlight. She wiped her hands on a towel and left the picking house. She could feel the men's eyes on her as she walked to her house, June close behind, the sound of her bare feet on the sand barely perceptible. A mother knows the sound of her own child, she thought.

"You get the basket and I'll get the shells," Clare said. She opened the cabinet and retrieved the large white enamel bowl her mother had brought over on the boat, the only boat to have landed at Timothy in fifty years. For years she'd waited for the boat to come back, as her parents had done, hoping that exile applied to only one generation.

But here she was, living in someone else's vacation home built centuries ago, the last of the books rank and spotted with mildew, food scarce, and many of the villagers suffering from malnutrition and melanomas. Here she was, trying to remember her mother's stories about shampoo, television, and shopping malls.

June, always compliant, had prepared the basket of food that morning: three roasted and salted gulls, five oranges, two jars of marmalade, and two bottles of boiled rainwater. June checked it over one last time, added another jar of marmalade, and scooped the handle over her shoulder.

Clare paused at the door of her home and took a deep breath, bracing herself. She reached for June's hand and squeezed it, their skin warm, their hands callused. As they stepped outside into the humid air, the village stared back at them from the fountain. They were talking — she heard bits and pieces of conversation about nori and oysters, a shark that had been spotted near the reef — but she couldn't help but notice the way the conversation died as the door of her house creaked open.

Clare could see Javier standing next to Summer Hutchison and her father, Jim, who managed the rainwater plant. She nodded at everyone and walked toward the fountain with the enamel bowl balanced on her hip. Without being told, June walked quickly down to the beach to set the food basket by the pile of driftwood and rope, knowing instinctively that there wouldn't be time after the lottery.

Clare looked down at her daughter's silhouette on the beach, skinny and browned, long auburn braid hanging down her back. June had placed the basket next to the driftwood but was staring at Hope House, a distant, skeletal structure falling into the ocean, standing on rickety posts as waves crashed against the front door at high tide. The second summer of exile a big storm had come and taken the easternmost end of the island and a row of waterfront homes on the central beach, and Hope House, nearly a mile offshore, was all that remained of East Timothy. No one boated or swam out there anymore; the fishing was good, but the sharks were numerous and the boats weren't reliable.

"Let's move on with it, Clare," Jim Hutchison said.

Clare was thinking about how the big storm happened the year that the elders decided there were too many mouths to feed. She looked up at Jim. There was the sound of wingbeats and the black swarm of dragonflies moved over them, there and gone as they often were. The sound jarred her into the present.

"We'll take our time," Clare said, setting the bowl on the edge of the fountain. She wanted to keep proceedings calm; it was the only way to avoid a dangerous frenzy, to maintain control.

"Easy for you to say — you're exempt!" Huck Sleeman said, one tattooed arm around Jade. Lela played at their feet with a doll made of seaweed, sticks, and a square from an old quilt.

It was true. Clare's mother, Jennifer, had saved the exiles with agriculture. She'd coaxed saltwater rice paddies, orange trees, and surprising gardens from the island, which she tended to with rainwater and burlap guards to reduce salt burns. While the men had wasted their time building a boat that would never be seaworthy, Jennifer had accepted their plight and started the women's co-op, outlining a rigorous fishing schedule. She was a midwife, a nurse, a leader, and because of her contributions to an improved life on Timothy, Clare and June were exempt from the lottery, and their matriarchal line was considered the closest thing the island had to a monarchy. Being exempt from the lottery was a relief but it was also a burden, a guilty feeling, and Clare had spent the last month filled with a sense of unease, hot and sleepless in her bed.

Jennifer. To even think of her mother's name harkened to a different time and a mainland no one but Bruce Haverford knew. Bruce with his long white beard and rambling stories about baseball. He was seventy-five now, and sat in his flimsy lawn chair with its rusted joints, waiting for her to start. She made eye contact with him as she unfolded the list. He nodded curtly.

"I'll start with the heads of households," she said. "When I call your name, each member of the household will draw a shell."

"Formalities," Huck said. Clare felt as though she could see a snarl on his face, and it reminded her of what she'd worried over in bed these last nights when she couldn't sleep: how precarious her position was here on the island, her daughter's. What if people decided they wanted a new way? All she had on her side was tradition. Not brute force, not divine right, and luck — God, to speak of luck on this island was to lie. No one here knew luck, save for a good fishing day.

Just as Clare turned to offer the first shell

she saw Summer's mother, Beth Hutchison, hurrying up the sandy path to the village square, her thick gray hair held back by a red scarf. She held her youngest daughter Kate's hand. Beth locked arms with Jim and touched Summer on the back. "I let the day get away from me," she whispered. "I forgot. How could I forget?"

Javier nodded at Beth politely. His eyes returned quickly to Summer. He was thinking of the hushed nights when he had come to her in the shallow, dark water and they'd stood there alone looking out at the dim horizon. She worried about her future, as they all worried, and he assured her that if things got bad she could make it on her own, that he would come join her, that nothing could keep her from him. He reached for her hand and held it tightly.

"Thought we'd have to start without you, Beth," Jade said.

"Kate and I were just hanging up the last of the laundry!" she said. "You wouldn't want us all to be wandering around naked tomorrow."

There was polite laughter, but it died down quickly.

"Some of us have to get back to work, Clare," Huck muttered.

"Anderson," Clare called out. "Who's

drawing for Anderson?"

"I am," a woman said, reaching for the shell. She didn't dare peek at whatever was carved into the white, pearlescent inside. She cupped the shell facedown in her hand and receded into the crowd.

"Bentham," Clare said. "Bentham," she repeated when no one came up.

"He's sick," Huck said from the back. "Laid up with some gut problem."

"Someone has to draw for him," Clare said. She tried to keep an emotionless face, a fair face.

"Fine," Huck said, weaving through the crowd, reaching into the bowl. He held the shell up then laid it facedown on the fountain. "This one here's for Bob."

"Bruce Haverford," Clare said, thinking to herself: dear Bruce. Last of my mother's friends. Last of the original exiles. It was a dubious distinction, she thought. She loved him for his age and experience, and yet wasn't he part of the reason they were here?

Javier helped Bruce rise from his chair and kept one arm on him until he was steady. Bruce shuffled toward the bowl, reached in for a shell with a solemn face, and retreated. "Thirty years," he said to himself. "Thirty years I've done this."

Clare moved down the list of names:

"Hutchison, Jackson, Sleeman."

"Go on, now, Huck," Jade said. "The moment you've been waiting for." Each member of the family took a shell. Jade held on to Lela's.

"It seems like we just had a lottery, doesn't it?" Beth whispered to Summer, who was still clutching Javier's hand.

"Lewis."

"Get up there, boy," someone said. Javier dropped Summer's hand and went to claim his shell. He was an orphan, the last of his family. Sometimes that gave him the feeling that he was lucky, that he'd had his share of misfortune when it came to the lottery. He worked hard to be a trusted, valuable member of Timothy.

June stood next to her mother, silent, and watched Javier. She thought he was beautiful, and sometimes she hated Summer for having his attention the way she did. The other boys were young, too young.

"Who's ready for a residency at the Hope House?" Huck asked, smiling stupidly with his bad teeth. But no one laughed. "Shut up," Jade hissed. "Just be quiet for once."

"Sleep on the second floor," he said. "Spear fish from the front door. That's my plan. Don't worry about me when it's my turn to go."

"Shut up," Jade said again.

You could hear someone scream from the Hope House, June thought. She'd learned that last year. That was the part she really hated. Or when people tried to come back. When people made it close to shore, all starved and raving mad.

You could see the shells burning holes in people's hands, Clare thought. It had always been this way, ever since the first time her mother had read the names. What if we just tried to get by? Outlawed children and died out gracefully? she wondered. But you couldn't keep people from getting pregnant, and they had to allow themselves the consolations of joy, didn't they? That had been her mother's thinking.

"We won't have to do this much longer," someone said. "Next big storm and the ocean will wash right over us."

What if they turn on me? Clare was thinking. What if the system fails?

"Watson . . . Zanini . . . ," she read.

Javier was thinking about how he'd build his boat with the driftwood. You had thirty minutes to make a boat, and then the shells started coming at your head. Just like everyone else on the island, he'd planned for a day like this. The current moved northwest. You could take the food basket and go, but everyone knew the waves were too much for a small raft, the current too strong. There was Hope House, but no one ever lasted at Hope House. No one had ever lasted.

"I wish you'd read the number," Beth said quietly.

Clare could hear the dragonflies. They weren't far away. She felt as if she was drifting in and out of her body. She felt as if her mother was inside of her, speaking for her, giving her the strength to do the right thing. The right thing, she repeated to herself.

Everyone was quiet because they knew it was time to turn over the shells. In a minute they would know.

Javier started to get a strange feeling in his heart, something dark and irritable, a feeling beyond sadness. Jade Sleeman lowered her gaze and began mumbling a prayer. None of them really knew how to pray but they'd been taught, and if they had not been taught they'd seen the exiles years ago bowing down in front of the driftwood cross, the one bleached by the sun and surrounded by semicircles of shells, which sometimes people kneeled upon until they bled.

No one moved, no one dared breathe until Clare raised her hand. All at once everyone exhaled except for Summer, who dropped her shell, the one that had the cross etched inside instead of a number. She began backing away from everyone, staring at them like a startled animal, nostrils flared, mouth open. Her mother fell to the ground, crying. "It isn't fair."

"Everyone took the same chance," Jade said, as her eyes followed Summer down to the beach. "It's always been this way."

"It's the way it has to be," Bruce said from his chair, rising. "There isn't a choice."

"Clare," Beth said, repeating the name over and over again.

June reached for Clare, but she was distant, thinking of her own mother, her scent, something like burned skin, cooked onions, and carrots fresh from the earth. She thought of her mother's sins, and the ways she paid for them. The way they all did.

Jim Hutchison crouched as if he might be sick. Someone handed his youngest daughter, Kate, a conch shell, an old one that had an exposed, cream-colored spiral. She looked at it, and then at her sister.

June moved forward, waiting. She'd never cared so much about a lottery. She'd never had such mixed feelings.

Javier stood at the front of the crowd, staring at the beach. Summer was already down there, working to build the driftwood raft, the basket of food by her side. He guessed that she had about twenty minutes left. Jim placed a hand on his shoulder, but Javier shrugged it off. He remembered something Summer had said one night as he held her weightless in the water, kissing her neck. Her legs were wrapped around his body, her pale hair long and loose, the moonlight glinting off her damp forehead, the skeleton of the Hope House on the horizon. She'd whispered, "Sometimes I think I'd rather die fast than go it alone and die slowly."

"But you wouldn't," he'd said. "Because I'd find you, and we'd make it. We'd get to the Hope House. We'd survive."

But as she looked up from the raft to find Javier's face, her fingers tying the wood together as they'd practiced, Summer saw something in his eyes, something he hadn't expected would be there himself, and she stood up from the pile of wood. She started back toward the village as she was not allowed to do, and it was an invitation. It was a request. Though she'd never seen a ballet in her life, she opened up her body like a dancer, arms out, eyes shut, and thrust her chest forward to willingly receive the rocks and shells that found it.

Tiny Davis **Photo reprinted with permission, copyright © Jezebel Productions, Inc.**

HELL-DIVING WOMEN

The bus driver quit last night, and Ruby is behind the wheel of Big Bertha again, going fifty down I-95 in the dark, the bus jostling and rattling over hot tar. It's late August, and even with the windows down the sweet, muggy air hangs over the women, heating the tops of their instrument cases, warming the expired cold cuts Tiny asks Ruby to keep in a bag behind the driver's seat so she can make sandwiches and sell them to the other girls for a profit. *I gotta hustle, baby,* she says, sending Ruby out to buy the meat at the nearest grocery store while the girls practice.

The band lives on the road, gig to gig. They stay up late, practice in the gymnasiums at colored schools, do each other's hair and makeup, call home if there's a home to call. The days are starting to run together, Ruby thinks. The nights at the clubs too.

How long can it go on? Ruby wonders.

291

Sure, there'll be an end. There always is — I just can't see it. Why work so hard? Why travel so much? We sure as hell ain't getting rich. We're getting tired.

Ruby blots her face with a handkerchief. She's thinking about Tiny as she drives, watching the cotton undulate as the big bus passes field after field. Last night Tiny started a set with her signature line: "I make my living blowing! Horns, that is." Ruby was having a drink — she was rarely on-stage, though she wanted to be — and heard the bartender mutter something about "that fat dyke on the trumpet." It hadn't set well with her. She'd gritted her teeth, started sweating, angry as hell. But she couldn't think of the right thing to say. No, she thinks. I *knew* the right thing to say but I didn't say it. Scared as a cat at the dog pound lately.

He don't know, Ruby thinks, shaking her head. Tiny's a prophet. A genius with no education. A lover and a fighter. A performer, through and through. Shit, man, Count Basie and the Duke want her on-stage. She's a star! She can hit a high C!

A foul smell finds its way into the bus window, the unmistakable smell of pigs, hot shit, and slop that's all over Carolina. Like rotten eggs. When the Yankee girls get to squishing up their noses about it, asking, "What's that smell?" Tiny is quick to say, "Smells like money to me." Ruby smirks. She's always Tiny's audience, not that she ever lacks one.

But no one is awake now. When it's this quiet, her ears ring. Too much horn. Too many drumbeats. It doesn't hurt when she plays, just when she listens. More playing then, she thinks, shaking her head a little.

It's just me and this long, flat road, Ruby thinks. This big blue moon.

She notices bread crumbs scattered across the bus floor from dinner; she'll sweep them up when they stop for breakfast. She can smell old smoke and the bandleader, Anna Mae Winburn's gardenia perfume, though Anna Mae has long taken off her white gown and plumed hat and fallen asleep in a berth with cold cream on her face.

Occasionally Ruby passes a farmhouse with the windows thrust open and a light on, and she wonders what people are doing up at three in the morning, if there are sleepless mothers with children or lovers fighting. There's laundry drying on the lines, the silhouettes of cows in the fields that remind her of the farm her grandfather worked on. More driving. More pine trees. It's so flat out here, she thinks.

There's a paper mill on the horizon, smoke billowing from its stack. She thinks of the people working the late shift. People like her father. And then she thinks of nothing at all, just gives herself over to the soothing vibration of the bus, the terribly slow bus, and smokes.

She likes smoking. They all do, even the pretty girls. Cigarettes are good for the jazz singer's voice; they smooth it out.

Someone taps Ruby on the shoulder. It's Rae Lee, the manager, lipstick still clinging to her lips in the middle of the night, peering at her through cat-eye glasses.

"Any trouble?"

Ruby exhales smoke out of the open window and clenches the cigarette between her teeth. "No trouble."

"Anyone ask you any questions?"

"No questions."

"We'll honor our commitments," Rae Lee whispers. "We won't upset the girls with details. Nervous girls are bad performers. Best to keep on, nail our gigs in Kinston and Rocky Mount, then head up 95 through Virginia and over past Washington, where we can rest for a few days away from Jim Crow. We can regroup and pick up some supplies."

"Yep," Ruby says, nodding slowly, eyes

fixed on the road. "Fine with me."

Rae Lee claps a hand on Ruby's shoulder, then turns and shuffles back to her seat in her new slippers. She's the only one with new slippers. "She's skimming off the pot every gig," Tiny has whispered to Ruby. Maybe it's true, Ruby thinks. But I'm not going to say *anything.* I'm going to look the other way. I'm lucky to be here. I'll do what I'm told.

Ruby is the do-anything girl. It's not the best job in the world, but it's a job that keeps her close to Tiny and close to music. She sets out dinner or runs errands to buy sanitary napkins and Coca-Cola when the girls practice. She loads and unloads luggage. If Pauline gets sick and can't play drums, Ruby plays drums. If Johnnie Mae needs a break from piano, which she hardly does, Ruby plays piano. And if the bus driver quits, and several have, because he's tired of running from the law, Ruby takes the wheel.

"I can't do it anymore," the driver said to Rae Lee last night. "I can't take sheriff after sheriff banging on the bus door every gig, asking if we have white and colored girls mixing. They *know* we do. Hell, we advertise it! America's first integrated all-girl swing band or whatever the hell you call it. I don't want to go to prison. I've got five grand-daughters."

"The police can't keep you," Rae Lee said, hand on hip.

"They can do anything. And if the police don't do it, you *know* who will if we keep talking about 'the blood of many races' and whatnot."

Ruby knew who the driver was talking about. She'd watched men walk right up to the bus, tucking vicious notes underneath the windshield wipers: *How can you sleep, eat, and work together? You disgust me. Leave town or you'll burn while you sleep.* Black, white, Jewish, Mexican, Asian, Hawaiian, mixed up — the International Sweethearts had it all. The girls were chased out of diners and gas stations, refused restrooms, had shop doors closed in their faces. And yet the lines of people still wrapped around the clubs every night, though when the gigs were over Ruby half-expected to see torches coming for the bus. She was always looking over her shoulder now. She was often left alone with the bus, or laundering uniforms in some back-alley place. If someone was looking to pick a fight or make a point, she was an easy target.

Not afraid to use that blade I keep in my back pocket, she thinks. Not above raking it down some man's face, especially if he's got a white pointy hat on.

Tiny had the Klan on Ruby's brain. Last night she got going about it as soon as she got the mic in front of her face. *When I think of the South — I think of something southern. Like magnolia blossoms . . . chittlins . . . hush puppies . . . and those three bad brothers, Klu, Kluck, and Klan.*

"You can't go talking about the KKK into a microphone," Rae Lee hissed when Tiny finished her second encore. "You can be funny but you can't be outrageous. You can't put us all in danger like that."

"You've got to entertain or go home," Tiny says, shrugging Rae Lee off. "You gotta take the audience someplace."

"You've got to keep it *clean.*"

"I'm giving them *all* of me. Take it or leave it, baby."

No one was going to leave it and Tiny knew as much, Ruby thinks. Sure the band is hot right now, but it's Tiny that gets the people on their feet. When Anna Mae's pretty ballads are done and Tiny gets up there all fat and loud with her horn, people go crazy.

Ruby hears footsteps behind her. *Finally,* she thinks, smiling as she catches Tiny's eyes in the rearview mirror. This is the high point of every long night. Tiny in her cheetah-print silk pajamas and wrapped hair wandering to the front of the bus, two hundred and thirty pounds but quiet as a panther when she wants to be.

Tiny crouches over her shoulder and whispers in her ear. "You and me, baby. We're going to break off from these uptight girls and do our own thing. Vegas for a while. The seediest clubs in Brooklyn. Just bide our time and then we'll jump."

"Yeah," Ruby says, heart beating fast. "I'd like that." Ruby knows Tiny is all talk, all hustle, keeping her options open, but God, it feels good to think about having her to herself, living a little lighter, a little faster. Managing themselves, their time, their songs.

Tiny squeezes Ruby's shoulder. The tips of her fingers rest on Ruby's skin, but only for a few seconds; she's gone again. Rae Lee and the girls know about Tiny and Ruby, but they don't want to see it. They know but they don't *know*.

It was no small thing, driving that bus. It was hard on her nerves. Even tonight, even when the bus can't exceed the speed limit, Ruby waits for the blue lights in the window. Maybe someone will wake up soon and keep her company. Or maybe there will be more hours like this, alone, her hands on the wheel.

Ruby pulls the bus into a quiet-looking Gulf station around six in the morning in a little town called Dunn. The station is small but rambling, as if it used to be a house and has been added on to and forgotten throughout the years. The windows are dirty and there are signs for dry goods, notions, and oil changes. A few crows caw from the red tin roof, and cicadas are going in the dense brush surrounding the place.

"Dunn ain't nothing but sticks and dip," Tiny mutters, surveying the scene as she exits the bus onto the gravel lot. "Guess y'all gon' have to buy my sandwiches."

Ruby always stops places where you can't buy much, because it's better for Tiny's business. Tiny doesn't have to ask.

Sixteen girls plus Rae Lee and Ruby file out of the bus, most of them in sleeveless cotton shifts, hopelessly wrinkled until they find a place to iron. While the girls brush their teeth in the woods and stretch their legs, Ruby sets out seventeen folding chairs, then a card table with bread, jam, and instant coffee. She works fast, swigging black coffee between tasks.

"Get your damn shoes on," Rae Lee tells

Johnnie, the pianist. She's last to get off the bus, and her eyes are sleepier than usual. She coughs into her hand. Johnnie, like half of the girls, comes from the Piney Woods School, a place for colored orphans. Right off the Mississippi farm, they'd all learned to play on banged-up instruments. Some of them had been on the road since they were sixteen. They didn't know any different, only that life on the bus was better than what they'd been trained for, which was pretty much cleaning house and sewing.

"Nobody's watching," Tiny says, the only one brave enough to talk back to Rae Lee. "There's no audience here." But Johnnie has already run back onto the bus for her shoes and reemerges, still bleary-eyed. Ruby hands her coffee in a Styrofoam cup, and Johnnie takes a sip, wincing.

She looks sick, Ruby thinks. *Please* be sick. God forgive me for these thoughts, but I want to get up on that stage and play.

Johnnie sneezes and wipes her nose on her elbow.

"Johnnie Mae, are you able to play tonight?" Rae Lee asks. "Ruby can stand in."

"Johnnie's fine," Tiny snaps. "Let her be."

Ruby turns away, then boards the bus. She stands next to the driver's seat, one hand on the pockmarked leather, heart pounding.

Why did Tiny's words feel like a betrayal? She's just standing up for Johnnie, Ruby thinks, opening her eyes wide then blinking to rid them of the tears threatening to fall.

You're not a crying woman, she tells herself, just as her own mother used to. You're a patient woman. Hardworking. So get out there and work.

That afternoon they arrive in Kinston, Ruby steering the bus to a spot behind the armory. The girls are already in their dresses and jackets, hair curled, their faces made up for the Tobacco Festival. The brass instruments are shined and the sheet music is organized. Anna Mae sits away from the fray in her white column gown, trying to stay clean. Her eyes are closed, but Ruby can see her lips moving, practicing her set. Further back Tiny is running through finger exercises, her trumpet silent, her fingers arched and limber.

"We're going to start with 'Jump Children,'" Rae Lee is saying at the front of the bus, clipboard in hand. "And if anyone gets to asking you about what race you are, you just smile and pretend you can't hear a word, understand?"

As the girls file out of the bus, Ruby bringing up the rear, she can smell barbecue, hear the twangy vocals coming from the festival's center stage. A line of food carts and tobacco vendors flanks the railroad tracks. Men in coveralls stand over amber-colored bales of tobacco, auctioneers fast-talking their way into sales.

God, I'm tired, she thinks. Just a two-hour nap and another long night ahead.

A crowd is gathering on Main Street for the parade, bunched in front of the old Paramount Theater, children on shoulders. A blue balloon goes free from a child's loose fingers, lifting up and further up still, into the warm air.

There's a bandstand waiting for the Sweethearts, a series of white music stands and boxes, and they know how to make it work; they can make anything work. They file in and tune up. To Ruby this is a painful wheeze of a sound, a breathing in before you can breathe out. The cymbals shake. Vi and Roz run the scales on the sax. Anna Mae gives the cue and turns to the crowd with her soprano:

When you're feelin' low and you don't know what to do . . .

Soon a truck creeps slowly toward the stage with a white float hitched to the back. Ruby cranes her neck to see a young white girl in a sparkling white bathing suit. She has a crown on her head, long brown hair cascading down her shoulders, and she's waving, one arm around a large white plastic deer. The ribbon around her neck reads: "Miss Tobacco Queen, 1944." She's surrounded by girls in high heels perched on top of tobacco bales, waving brown, crinkled leaves like handkerchiefs.

We're too good for this, Ruby thinks. Too good.

"Little white girl with a plastic deer," Tiny says, leaning into the mic after the song is finished. "How about that. A round of applause for that pretty girl and her deer."

Ruby takes a sharp breath. Did anyone notice Tiny's disdain?

"Can't Help Lovin' Dat Man." "Sweet Georgia Brown." "Lady Be Good." Soon the set is finished, the sun has faded, and the girls are whisked away for drinks at a fancy house down the road. There's a white man in a nice suit talking to Rae Lee. "Bring your instruments!" he says, grinning.

"Can't just visit," Tiny mutters. "Gotta work for you, huh?"

Ruby looks at Johnnie's face, then Pauline's. The girls are tired, but Rae Lee's answer is always the same. Yes.

"Someone's got to stay here and clean up," Rae Lee says.

"Ruby has it under control," Tiny says.

And so, as the girls follow the man in the nice suit with all the instruments they can carry, Ruby does as she always does. She takes down the drum kit, wipes it clean, loads it into the bus. She folds the stands and files away the music. One last night on the road, she thinks, and then a motel. Finally, a motel.

She isn't old, but her bones ache and her head hurts, mostly from sleep deprivation. As she moves from the bus to the bandstand, she catches sight of a man in her peripheral vision, a man in a not-so-nice suit and a brown cap. He comes closer, and closer, until finally she wipes her hands on her pants and asks him, "Can I do something for you?"

"There's a white girl in that band," he says. "Ain't there."

Ruby shrugs. "Who knows?" she says, moving back toward the bandstand. But he grabs her arm. "*You* know," he says.

Ruby pulls away, but she doesn't dare speak. Speaking is inviting trouble. They stand there like that at an impasse, the festival quieting down behind them, bales of tobacco being packed away, the pungent golden scent still lingering in the air.

"I don't know where you're from," he

says. "But we do things differently down here. We don't mix. It ain't allowed."

"I understand," Ruby says, backing away.

"We'll make you understand," he says. Ruby waits for more, but there isn't any more, not tonight. She drives the bus back to the armory, folds her arms across her chest, and waits for sleep that doesn't come.

She's driving again, back on 95, almost always 95. Nodding off, jolting upright, pinching her face, biting her fingers to stay awake. Just another half hour and she can park in Rocky Mount. Just another half hour and she can stop having a conversation with herself.

What am I good for? she wonders.

A lot of things. I can play music by ear. *But you can't read it.*

I can learn it quickly. *But you can't perfect it. If you could, you'd be on that stage, not driving this bus.*

Who cares about me? *Tiny does, sometimes.*

Rae Lee settles into the seat behind her, yawning. "Too much champagne," she says, touching her temples.

Ruby grits her teeth.

"Any trouble?" Rae Lee asks.

"A little," Ruby says.

305

"Not the law?"

"Just another man upset that we've got white girls onstage. Upset about mixing."

Rae Lee nods. "We'll get through tonight, rest, and then next month we'll be back at the clubs. It's safer at the clubs. They don't mind so much."

"The good ones don't," Ruby says. She opens and closes her jaw, trying to wake up. Sweat drips down her back. She presses on.

The band is due onstage at the Cotton Ball in one hour, and Roz, the Jewish girl from up north, is a mess. She's looking at herself in the bathroom mirror, frowning, lip quivering.

"Here," she says, handing Tiny a compact with dark foundation in it. "I want you to put this on my face."

"Not me," Tiny says, walking away, holding up a hand. "I don't want nothing to do with that business."

"Someone," Roz says, tears in her eyes. "Help."

Pauline steps up and wipes a sponge through the dark makeup. "Here you go," she says. "Just don't get worked up now and smudge things."

Tiny comes closer to have a look. "I know you mean well," she says. "But you're awfully hard to look at."

"All the better," Roz says, sniffling. "I don't want anyone to notice me. I don't want to get anyone in trouble. Not tonight."

Rae Lee, for once, doesn't have anything to say. She watches the girls over her cat-eye glasses from the corner of the dressing room, then looks back down at the set list on the clipboard.

"You and me next year," Tiny whispers to Ruby. "Bad as we are, on the road, no crying."

Ruby nods her head, rocking a little on her stool as she laughs. She likes her laugh, low and throaty. It's a jazz singer's laugh, even if she's not much of a singer.

"Could you put some tea on?" Rae Lee asks Ruby. "Girls, have a little tea before the set. We want to do our best, see if we can get this gig next year. It's worth two nights at the club, if you know what I mean."

After preparing tea, Ruby heads out in front of the band to lay down the sheet music. The ballroom is beautiful. There are white flower arrangements everywhere, white lights, white linens, white tufts of cotton, white marble. White, white, and more white.

Moments later the girls file onstage as a short man in a crisp suit hollers, "The best of the Big Band era! Right here in Rocky Mount! On your feet for the International Sweethearts of Rhythm!"

Ruby watches the girls flesh out the bandstand in their white suits, waving politely in their nicest costumes, the ones they save for the best-paying gigs. There's thunderous applause, a sea of white faces in front of them, men with freshly combed hair, women in high heels and pearls. Mink stoles in summer. Ruby wants to be onstage and feels a part of herself go with the band. She imagines the ivory keys beneath her fingers.

Anna Mae, Hepburn-thin and elegant as ever, nods her head to the audience. She has a lush black feather in her hair, a white dress that wraps around her neck, and a brooch on her collar. "I have a question for you," she says into the microphone. "Do you want to jump tonight?"

The audience claps their hands. Someone whistles.

"I said do you want to jump, children?"

The audience roars and the trumpets kick into gear, the drums, the bass. The sax players turn their bodies in synced-up rhythm. The horns are loud and clear. God, it's a sort of high when they nail a song, Ruby thinks, really nail it. If only I could be part of that flow, part of that sound.

The night starts well, high energy like the best of them, but the crowd is full of hecklers, men yelling things like "Hey, sweetheart, up there on the drums," and "brown sugar."

Ruby feels unsettled. She can see everything registering in Tiny's eyes. Just get through it, she thinks. Just get through it and onto the bus and everything will be fine, just fine.

"When I think of something southern . . . ," Tiny begins.

Ruby starts to get nervous. Has Tiny been drinking? Maybe she's just tired. She gets tired sometimes.

"I think of corn bread, chittlins . . ."

Tiny isn't the kind of person who needs to drink. Or is she?

"Hey there, black girl!" a man in a blue suit shouts, huge smile on his face. He holds his drink up to toast Tiny, sloshing small, clear drops of gin onto the floor.

"Hey, fella," Tiny shouts, looking down and gesturing with her trumpet. "It's not about being black. It's not about being a girl, though I like girls. It's about playing your goddamn music. Blowing your goddamn horn."

"I don't mean no harm," he says, his face twisted into what Ruby thinks is false contrition. He ain't sorry, she thinks.

Anna Mae is moving for the microphone, but Tiny grips it. "Sure you don't," she says. "Just like your brothers Klu . . ."

Rae Lee heads for the stage, Ruby not far behind her. Vi rises from behind the bandstand. But the man gets to Tiny first. He leaps onto the stage and goes for her, pulling her off the side of the stage, his arms underneath hers, and suddenly he is dragging her large body. Tiny's heels make a terrible sound going across the dance floor. She's still clutching her trumpet.

Ruby tries to get there. And she does, just not in time to stop Tiny from smashing her trumpet into the man's face, flinging it backward, connecting again. Ruby gets there only in time to grab the trumpet before Tiny goes for his face a third time. Ruby knows once Tiny starts she won't stop, and if she doesn't stop —

What happens to women like us? Ruby thinks. Her back is sore. She's been sitting in the same position on the cement floor for a while, holding Tiny's head in her lap. She has a busted lip and a cut above her eye, and all they've given her to stop the bleeding is a dirty-looking rag.

Tiny sits up gingerly, touches her lip with

her fingers. "Two girls like us," she says, cracking a smile. "We can make it on our own."

Not in this world, Ruby thinks, but she's not in the mood to disagree. "We sure can, sugar," she says, sighing. "Grab your horn and let's try."

"We're going to do better than try. I can pack a joint."

"Well, grab your horn."

"Are you driving?"

"Find me a car," Ruby says, clasping her knees as if she's going to rise up and go somewhere. "Find me a car and I'll take you anywhere. Let's go to Chicago."

"I don't want to go to Chicago. I want to go to Memphis."

"Memphis then."

"Where's my horn, anyway?"

Ruby shrugs her shoulders and stands up. She doesn't know. The naked bulb hanging from the ceiling of the jail cell flicks on and off.

"Anybody got a cigarette?" Ruby asks through the bars.

The guard does, but he's eating a chicken sandwich. Ruby can smell it and she's starving, really starving. He throws one cigarette, and then another at her.

"But ain't nobody got a light," Tiny says,

cigarette already in her mouth. "Not for us."

"Sing for it," the guard says, laughing. "Give me a torch song."

"Not for you, baby," Tiny says. "Not for you."

She gets up and flops down on the single cot in the cell. There isn't any room for Ruby.

Got what I wished for, Ruby thinks, leaning against the cinder-block wall, which is strangely cool against her back. I'm finally alone with my girl. Got her all to myself.

Ruby closes her eyes and begins to drift away, the cigarette falling from her lips. It's been a long time since she's slept, a long time since she's fallen asleep without the roar of the road underneath her.

AUTHOR'S NOTE

Robert de Montesquiou once said of the painter Romaine Brooks that she was a "thief of souls" — perhaps this thieving is what happens when an artist uses a real subject as inspiration. The stories in this collection are born of fascination with real women whose remarkable lives were reduced to footnotes. Many of these women came to light only because of intrepid biographers like Carol Loeb Shloss, Joan Schenkar, Kate Summerscale, and Meryle Secrest, who sourced photographs, letters, and interviews before they were lost to time.

I've never been comfortable with writing historical fiction, though I love reading it. When forming these stories, I kept with me Henry James's notion that all novelists need freedom, and I gave myself permission to experiment, and to be honest about my inspiration. These were stories I wanted to unlock from my imagination after a decade of reading and research. I wanted to talk about these women; I daydreamed about their choices as I was building my own life, one that seemed tame in comparison. I did not want to romanticize these women or dwell in glittering places; I'm more interested in my characters' difficult choices, or those that were made for them. I'm fascinated by risk taking and the way people orbit fame. I wanted to explore the price paid for living dangerously, such as undiagnosed post-traumatic stress disorder in women who served in World War I.

Suffice it to say, the world has not always been kind to its unusual women — though I did not intend these stories to serve as cautionary tales.

While I absorbed facts about these women's lives, I did not stay inside the lines; each of these stories is unequivocally a work of fiction. The women at the heart of my stories lived. And in my imagined events I have drawn upon their real lives and personalities and involved a few of their famous friends and lovers. I have, however, placed them in events and surrounded them with characters of my own creation. I'm indebted to the following resources for planting the seeds that became stories:

The Pretty, Grown-Together Children: I heard a whisper or two about the Hilton twins while living in North Carolina, then came across an entry about them on Roadside America.com.

The Siege at Whale Cay: I devoured Kate Summerscale's incredible, must-read biography of Joe, *The Queen of Whale Cay.* Further research has led me to the exceptional *Time Life* photoshoot of Joe and Whale Cay, as well as videos of Joe's races, which can be found at http://www .britishpathe.com/search/query/carstairs. I also found inspiration, though not philosophical agreement, in Helen Zenna Smith's novel about the female war experience, *Not So Quiet . . .*

Norma Millay's Film Noir Period: A friend turned me on to Nancy Milford's biography of Edna St. Vincent Millay, *Savage Beauty,* and like many young women I was perhaps, at first, fascinated more by her biography than by her work. When I was a resident at the Millay Colony for the Arts at Steepletop in 2007, I became acquainted with the wild stories about Edna's sister Norma, and found myself returning to her in my imagination, particularly the fact that she was an actress in her own right, with the renowned Provincetown Players, and inhabited her sister's estate for decades. Norma was a true force, and it was her presence I felt so keenly at Steepletop. Other resources include Cheryl Black's *The Women of Provincetown,* Daniel Mark Epstein's *What Lips My Lips Have Kissed,* Edna St. Vincent Millay's *Collected Poetry,* and her *Collected Letters* edited by Allan Ross MacDougall.

Romaine Remains: I came across this haunted, unusual figure in many books about Paris: *Wild Heart* by Suzanne Rodriguez, *Sylvia Beach and the Lost Generation* by Noel Riley Fitch, but most important, Meryle Secrest's (out of print) biography of Romaine, *Between Me and Life,* titled after Romaine's sentiment that her dead mother stood between her and living happily. I have framed prints of Romaine's line drawings, which I cut from Whitney Chadwick's catalog of Romaine's work, *Amazons in the Drawing Room.* Chadwick points out an element of Romaine's work that made a deep impression on me — the unusual depiction of "heroic femininity."

Hazel Eaton and the Wall of Death: Let me be intellectually honest here — Internet rabbit hole.

The Autobiography of Allegra Byron: I first heard of Allegra when I studied at Oxford for a summer, and also read Benita Eisler's *Byron: Child of Passion, Fool of Fame.* Furthermore, Dolly Wilde's fascination with Byron and her similarities to his daughter are pointed out in *Oscaria,* the privately printed book of remembrances about Dolly. Both girls were given over to convents at an early age, which was not particularly unusual at the time but could not have been a welcome experience. Allegra's story took off in my head years later, after I had children of my own, and could get more inside the head of a toddler.

Expression Theory: I saw a stunning photograph of Lucia Joyce in a hand-sewn costume, which led me to Carol Loeb Shloss's biography, *Lucia Joyce: To Dance in the Wake.* I found myself curious about the moment family members decided Lucia was deeply troubled; throwing the chair took on significance.

Saving Butterfly McQueen: I don't remember how I first heard of Butterfly, but when I found out that the *Gone With the Wind* star was an atheist, and had hoped to donate her body to science, I was intrigued, and couldn't help but imagine the waves of patronizing conversation she must have endured.

Who Killed Dolly Wilde?: Joan Schenkar's biography of Dolly Wilde, *Truly Wilde,* opened a door in my imagination, perhaps because she invited her readers to do just that, ending the introduction this way: "I have only been able to bring her to you complete with missing parts. It remains for you to do what Dolly could have done so beautifully for us all: Imagine the rest." Other sources include *Oscaria,* the private volume of recollections Natalie Barney had printed in Dolly's memory, which I am thankful for Bennington Librarian Oceana Wilson's help in obtaining access to. Additionally, Neil McKenna's *The Secret Life of Oscar Wilde* and Richard Ellmann's biography.

A High-Grade Bitch Sits Down for Lunch: When my mother-in-law passed away in 2009, it took me two years to read her favorite book, *West with the Night.* My mother-in-law was brave and athletic, a horsewoman, a young pilot, and a motorcycle-driving veterinarian — like Beryl Markham, a boundary breaker. I now teach Beryl's memoir, and celebrate the fact that it's one of the few books where we see a woman portrayed as an active hero of her own adventures with the absence of a central love story. While Beryl was a record-breaking pilot and author (not without authorship controversy, mind you), she was also Africa's first female certified horse trainer, a feat that required grit, fearlessness, and athleticism. I like to see women working in literature, using their bodies.

I also read biographical work on Markham from Mary S. Lovell and Errol Trzebinski, as well as Juliet Barnes's *The Ghosts of Happy Valley.*

The Internees: While researching an article about environmentalism and makeup, I came across an anecdote about the boxes of lipstick from Lieutenant Colonel Mervin Willett Gonin, who helped liberate the Bergen-Belsen concentration camp in 1945. Later, a friend, Henry Frechette, sent me the picture of Banksy's visual reinterpretation of the internees wearing lipstick. This, to me, is an unpretty and profound take on fame and femininity.

The Lottery, Redux: I was asked by Mc-

Sweeney's to write a "cover story" of a classic, and I chose Shirley Jackson's "The Lottery," because it's the first short story I remember reading, and I drive past her house in Bennington often. I knew I wanted to give homage to it with a matriarchal lineage in mind, and the idea that we pay for the mistakes our forebears make.

Hell-Diving Women: Oxford American asked me to write an essay on the International Sweethearts of Rhythm for their annual music issue. I had the pleasure of losing myself in research, and then finding out that the band played long ago in my hometown of Rocky Mount, North Carolina. After the article I found myself still dwelling on the material, and wanting to write a story. For further research, see D. Antoinette Handy's (out of print) biography on the Sweethearts and Jezebel Productions's short documentary *Tiny and Ruby: Hell-Divin' Women* (the name of Tiny and Ruby's post–World War II band).

There are other books which have enriched my imagination, including but not limited to: *Becoming Modern: The Life of Mina Loy* by Carolyn Burke; *The Well of Loneliness* by Radclyffe Hall; *Women of the Left Bank* by Shari Benstock; *Nightwood* and *Ladies Almanack* by Djuna Barnes.

ACKNOWLEDGMENTS

Thanks to the editors and journals who published these stories, particularly David Haglund at PEN, Caitlin Horrocks and David Lynn at *The Kenyon Review,* Sven Birkerts and Bill Pierce at *AGNI,* Dave Daley at *FiveChapters,* Desiree Andrews, formerly of *Tin House,* Beth Staples at *Ecotone,* and Daniel Gumbiner at *McSweeney's.*

My gratitude to my phenomenal agent, Julie Barer, and the rest of Team Barer, William Boggess and Gemma Purdy, who are as talented as they are supportive. Thanks to my brilliant editor and friend, Kara Watson, and the rest of the Scribner team, for being enthusiastic about another round of stories.

And all kinds of thanks to my family, particularly Mom, Dad, Emily, Evans, Sarah, John, Bob, and the rest of my tribe in Shaftsbury, like Tammy and Kathy, who help keep the ship afloat. It is a strange and beautiful ark, with toothless cats and old dogs.

To my husband, Bo, thank you for your equanimity, support, and love. And my ferociously smart daughters, Frasier and Zephyr, there is very little peace in your toddler ways, but endless inspiration. We are bolder together.

ABOUT THE AUTHOR

Megan Mayhew Bergman grew up in Rocky Mount, North Carolina, and attended Wake Forest University. She has graduate degrees from Duke University and Bennington College. Her first collection, *Birds of a Lesser Paradise,* was one of *Huffington Post*'s Best Books of 2012. Her work has appeared in *The New York Times, The Best American Short Stories, New Stories from the South, Ploughshares, Tin House,* and *Oxford American,* among other publications. She is the recipient of the 2015 Garrett Award for fiction from the Fellowship of Southern Writers.

She writes a sustainability column for *Salon* and lives on a small farm in Vermont with her veterinarian husband and two daughters.